I'll Be Right Here

I'll Be Right Here

Amy Bloom

GRANTA

Granta Publications, 12 Addison Avenue, London W11 4QR

First published in Great Britain by Granta Books in 2025

First published in the United States in 2025 by Random House,
an imprint and division of Penguin Random House LLC, New York.

Grateful acknowledgment is made to W. W. Norton & Company, Inc. for permission to reprint
"Here & Now" from *Briefings: Poems Small and Easy* by A. R. Ammons, copyright © 1971
by A. R. Ammons. Used by permission of W. W. Norton & Company, Inc.

A CIP catalogue record for this book is available from the British Library.

1 3 5 7 9 10 8 6 4 2

ISBN 978 1 78378 802 6 (hardback)
ISBN 978 1 80351 318 8 (trade paperback)
ISBN 978 1 78378 804 0 (ebook)

Book design by Susan Turner
Offset by Iram Allam

Printed and bound by CPI Group (UK) Ltd, Croydon, CR0 4YY

The manufacturer's authorised representative in the EU
for product safety is Authorised Rep Compliance Ltd,
71 Lower Baggot Street, Dublin D02 P593, Ireland.
www.arccompliance.com

www.granta.com

For W.A.M.

. . . or music heard so deeply
That it is not heard at all, but you are the music
While the music lasts.

—T. S. ELIOT, *Four Quartets*

Here & Now

Yes but
it's October and the leaves
are going
fast: rain weighted
them and then
a breeze
sent them in shoals clear across
the street

revealing
especially in the backyard
young maple
branch-tip buds that assume
time as far away as
the other side of the sun

—A. R. Ammons

Contents

Alma and Anne are holding Gazala's hands.

Alma massages in the neroli oil Gazala likes. Honey rolls off Gazala's fluffy slippers and massages the oil into her thin feet. The room smells like roses and orange peel.

Death circles through Gazala's blood, in her bowels, into her bones.

"It is eating me," Gazala says. "Make it stop."

"I know," Alma says. "You want to sit up?"

Anne comes around to the other side of the bed, to help. Honey puts down the oil and picks up a pillow to put under Gazala's knees if Gazala wants to sit up.

Gazala nods.

"Ice chips," Honey says. Alma and Anne look at each other. Help or harm? Anne and Alma shrug.

Honey goes to the kitchen and comes back with a Tupperware bowl filled with ice chips.

Samir is sitting where Honey sat. He presses his hand over his mouth so that he will not cry out at the sight of his dying sister, surrounded by her sisters. Honey puts her hand on his shoulder, and he inclines his head toward her hand. Habibi, he says. Darling.

Anne pulls up the shade. The day is beautiful. Gazala turns her face away from the light, and Alma pulls the shade back down.

Gazala hears Samir sigh. She tilts her head toward him and opens her eyes. They see each other.

Samir says, to Alma, Anne, and Honey, "My dears, please come back later."

Gazala sighs. She closes her eyes. She has lost the thread.

The red thread Gazala pulls, the raised embroidery she feels between her fingertips, is her father pouring tea for her, Samir leaning out the window to watch two boys kick a ball.

PART ONE

Then

Gazala

Me, Myself, Gazala

It is the first thing I remember.

I am lying on my side, on the woven straw mat, pulling at the red stitching. The mat is scratchy and thin under me, and at the edge of my feet the packed dirt of the courtyard is hard. Samir rolls a bead necklace toward me, to play with. Two dogs piss against the wall, the short yellow streams running down the darkened wall. I sit up in a wide bar of light, and the rest of the courtyard is cool, green in the corners at the edge of the brown brick. The cement sticks out like thick dirty cream. My father says that the workmen were no good, they were *en désordre,* and he added an Algerian word I don't know. When I run my thumb over the cement, over the tiny sharp peaks, it sticks me and I cry out. My brother drags me by the foot back to the mat. I crawl as far as the brick and the irresistible white dirtiness, and Samir lures me back with blue and green glass beads sliding and clicking on a leather string. He hides them under the mat, in his pockets, under his feet. The beads are in my mouth or dangling above me, sparkling in the light. The light comes and goes all day.

I climb into my brother's lap, and he pulls the mat over me. It gets a little colder, and Samir lays me on top of his legs to warm us both, and then, then as the light fails, our father comes home.

The makroud from our father's pockets are a little stale and a little dusty, but there are two for each of us and he is too tired to care if we eat sweets before dinner or not. Sometimes he brings home cinnamon montecaos, seeping oil into the twist of paper. We lick the paper. We eat the green beans, when there are green beans, and our father puts shreds of lamb, folded in bread, into my hand. I eat from my father's hand until I'm bigger and then from my own hand when I'm four, when he's sure that I won't drop the plate. We have six plates. We have four cups. We have four glasses. We have one beautiful thing, which is my mother's tin teapot, a berrad, with leaves and flowers etched on the tin.

We have two beds, one for our father and one for us, and when I am seven and Samir is eleven, our father finds an actual mattress for himself and Samir, wide enough for the two of them, and we switch. My father doubles my bedding in the other corner and adds another blanket because I won't have Samir to keep me warm.

On Sunday my father pulls out the newspaper, a copy left behind by a morning customer. He rattles it open. He clears his throat. Sometimes, to make the suspense more delicious,

more delightful, like being tickled, but only just enough, by
someone who truly loves you, he pauses and says: Let's have
some tea. He makes a cup for himself and for Samir, and he
lets me take sips from his cup.

Where was I?, he says.

Ah, yes. I see here in the paper . . . He rattles the paper
again and lifts it to cover his face so that all I can see is the
French newspaper down to his blue corduroy trousers and
his worn Algerian slippers. He does have French slippers
too, cracked brown leather.

I see here in the paper, my father says, that one of the
most beautiful lions from the Zoo de Ben Aknoun—I'm sure
you remember that, Samir . . . And Samir nods, although he
was only a month old when his mother died and my parents
became his parents. All he knows of Algeria is what I know,
is what we've heard from the old man who has a small room
on the other side of the courtyard and who speaks a little
Darija to our father and seems to have been dying since I
was born.

Samir knows the names of the cookies and the flattened
dates we eat at the end of the day. He sometimes rubs our
mother's teapot against his shirt, to brighten it, and he tells
me, when he's angry, that he remembers everything about
my mother, the woman who became his mother, too. Her
curly brown hair, he says. Not black like yours, but brown
like dark honey. Her hands were like white butterflies, he
says, and then he shakes his head. You don't remember anything, he says—

Our father rattles the newspaper. It says here that one of

the most beautiful lions, as beautiful as the great bronze lions
that guard the great mosque of Oran . . .

We nod.

I say: A *Barbary* lion, from the royal palace. I get a nod
and a cookie from behind the newspaper.

Indeed, he says. A Barbary lion. The greatest lions of
Algeria. As I say, I see here that the lion had been roaming
the streets of Oran with a man—a Berber, is what I understand. Maybe his name was Samir, he says, and he winks at
Samir. Maybe, he says, who knows, the newspaper doesn't
give a name, maybe it was a girl *dressed* as a man. A skinny
girl, she put on rags and a great black beard, and maybe it
was she who walked the streets of Oran with a lion. Our
father makes a face at me.

So, he says. A wanderer.

We shrug. We are city people, is what my father gives us
to understand. We are not and were not nomads. We are
descended from exceptional people, superior Muslims and
Christians both, and a rabbi, he said. You see how close the
words are: the name Rabee, your great-uncle was Rabee,
and the word *rabbi*—all tributes to the mutafawiq river of
education and understanding that flows in our very veins.
So, this Berber—I don't see a name, my father says—has
been pulling that old stunt, getting the simple folk to pay him
so that his lion doesn't eat them. You know that one, he says
to Samir, who nods like he has been fleecing simple folk and
laughing up his sleeve since he could walk.

Well, it was unusual, my father says. The lion was obviously very clever. He was trained to roar and frighten the

village folk, and then the Berber collected food, maybe a little money, from the people, fed the lion a lamb, and if not they split a tagine jelbana, is what I think, my father says, and then they moved on. Not a bad trick. But I see here that after a couple of months of village folk and lamb dinners, the lion *ate* the Berber.

We gasp.

Poor man. Worse and worse, my father says. The lion reveals himself to be not the docile companion of a Berber charlatan, not a servant content with bits of lamb and a pat on the head, but a proud—and hungry—killer. Our father reads silently for a few seconds.

Aha. Ahh. I see.

If we sit still, he will continue. We know he will but it is agonizing to hold ourselves tightly, not to give him a tap on the knee.

More tea, Baba?, I say. My father says nothing. He clears his throat.

Extraordinary. It says here that the lion leapt through El Hamri onto a freighter just leaving the Harbor of Oran. Our beautiful harbor, he says. It hugs the city and then sweeps out to the Mediterranean, blue like nothing here in France, never.

We press our feet up against each other's. We clasp hands.

Onto a freighter. Remarkable. What a creature this lion must be. A mane like the blazing sun, paws bigger than melons, teeth, can you imagine, teeth like giant knives. It says here that the International Crime Police were notified. *The*

International Crime Police! They seem to have tracked the lion to . . . Well, it says here that they tracked him to Europe. The lion disembarked in France, my father says. I'm a little puzzled by this, he says, but it seems to say that the lion came into Paris, into the tenth arrondissement, that he came down rue La Fayette.

But this cannot be, my father says.

The lion's picking up speed.

It says that the lion came down rue La Fayette and turned left onto rue de la Charbonnière to rue Caplat, traveled another little bit and turned into a courtyard, and it says here that the lion went down the street, turned right through a brick archway, and aywah, aywah, aywah, AND . . . HERE . . . HE . . . IS!

He drops the newspaper to the floor and roars. We beat our feet on the floor and scream with pleasure.

Barbary Lion Escapes was our favorite game.

Our father, Mounir Benamar, is the sous-chef pâtissier, assistant to the pastry chef, of the good but not grand bakery Lefond et Fils. (The owner is the *fils*. The *père* died twenty years before, and the *fils* has no sons.) Lefond sells to people in the neighborhood, they sell day-old bread to the elderly, and they sell to the small bistro next door. No one travels across Paris for Lefond's almond croissants like they do for Pâtisserie Stohrer. (Samir says that Stohrer's croissants make Lefond's look like dogshit.)

Lefond makes regular, affordable baked things that regu-

lar French people like, and I like them too. They bake baguettes and brioches. They bake two-layer wedding cakes
with white fondant flowers (which taste like sugar and wax
and I am happy with every discolored rose petal and crumpled stem I get). My father says that they make entirely adequate Paris-Brest and Opéra cakes and macarons, éclairs
and mille-feuilles. When our father arrived at Lefond, he
offered to make some Algerian desserts, and they said: By all
means, bake away, but there's no need to call them Algerian.
People who knew knew, and they sold his ghriba cookies and
his walnut baklawa right next to the éclairs. I live on broken
éclairs and crushed macarons.

Lefond et Fils Pâtisserie has suffered in the war, almost
done in by the ration cards and M. Lefond's own decency.
(Mme. Lefond less so, Samir says.) The restaurants buy almost everything on the black market (sugar, ducks, rabbits,
legs of lamb, pork chops, coffee), but M. Lefond does not
understand the black market. He is too good. You can buy a
whole pig for 400 francs a kilo, if you have that kind of
money—and some people do. You can have sugar in your
coffee every day, if you have 150 francs for a kilo of sugar—
and some people do. M. Lefond does not, and he does not
grasp the point: Save yourself. He gives what he can to the
people who are hungry, he abides by the ration cards, and
when he cannot get enough sugar he stops making his famous raspberry cream macarons. He puts up a big sign: Pas
de macarons, next to the small sign that says: SoldatenKaf-
fee, which is to encourage German soldiers to come by. You
can't order a cup of coffee after three o'clock in a bistro, I

don't understand why, and if you can't have your coffee, you are not likely to order your madeleines or your sables, and so the bistro does not order dozens from Lefond et Fils. When you are at the Ritz you can buy coffee all evening and they still bring you a silver tower of cakes and petits fours at the end of the meal.

All around us, people we took for bumbling, honest folk more or less like ourselves reveal themselves to be criminal masterminds. The awful Mme. Odette, our concierge across the street, an old pile of rags herself, wrote a letter to the police about the Jews in the apartment on the third floor. (Who knew that she could even write? Samir said she might have had someone write it for her. In any case, we all knew it was her.) She took everything she could grab before the police came for the Jews at dinnertime and then returned a little later for the proper looting, with professional notebooks and official forms declaring that in the absence of the owners, the country of France would take possession of the contents of the apartment. Samir said it was called Möbel-Aktion and the Germans were furnishing their own homes with the things. The police brought burlap sacks and boxes for the clothes, the jewelry, the cigar case, the sewing machine, the needlepoint footstool. A man down the street, a piece of shit, Samir says, had been scrounging for years, selling single cigarettes and condoms, but when the Germans came to town he leapt up like Opportunity had not only knocked but thrown open the door and kissed him on the mouth. He sees what denouncing Jews can get you, which is not nothing, and then he has himself a little think, a serious talk with him-

self, and he begins looking for Jewish families who seem . . .
less obvious. Jewish grandmother? Recent baptism? Pretty
blond daughters with crosses the size of your thumb, but
what about the son with the curly brown hair and the nose
that does not, clearly does not, turn up at the tip?

Our father baked every day for fifteen years, up at three,
home by four. He fed us. He sheltered us and sent us to a
French school where we were mocked and abused but not
worse than the boy with the crossed eyes (spawn of the devil)
or the Romany children (filthy Gypsies) or the one truly Jewish girl (not half and half) who could have been my twin except for my little gold cross with the pearl in the center that
my father had found and pinned to my collar. My father
taught me to go to the corner store by myself and come
home unmolested, carrying the right things bought at the
right price and concealed in my six-pocket coat, which had
been his. He'd cut off ten inches of material, sewed two big
pockets into the lining, and added a scratchy tweed bib,
under the collar, to protect me from the cool Paris rain. He
showed me how to mend and patch everything we owned,
and today he cut up his oldest gabardine pants, so shiny in
the seat, Samir said, that you can see your face in it. He
opens every stitch and shows me, step by step, how to make
the pants into a dress. I wave the big scissors and he does the
work. He shreds the silk lining from around the waist and
makes a braided belt for me, not pretty but the right size.
And when he has done everything he can, he lies down on
the big mattress he shares with Samir and turns his face to
the wall.

We do not arrange for a proper burial. Samir says: We bury him, in our minds, in Oran. We tell the hateful Mme. Odette about our father, lying upstairs, and for a few coins she calls the authorities for us and they remove his body while, for another franc, we hide in her courtyard. We ask her to say that our father lived alone. I don't think any-one will come to bother us, but everyone knows orphans who find themselves kept by the Germans as toys or slaves and are then found dead in the Seine, or just crumpled and shoeless in the alley. (You cannot keep a pair of shoes in plain sight, in any neighborhood.) Samir left school without telling me, without complaint or notice, and showed up at the bakery the next morning, wearing my father's apron.

I wake up to an empty room and move over to the big mattress. I can pass for only twelve, with my hair in braids and a loose dress, which Samir thinks best, but it doesn't get me much. If Samir was not the sous-pâtissier, I would be a starveling like everyone else in the courtyard. He brings home whatever he can, in his pants and under his hat. He wraps two eggs in his scarf and tucks the scarf into his jacket. He puts half a baguette down his pant leg and limps home. He trades the bread for other things, on the way home, and walks in with a carrot and a green potato. We do share with the courtyard for a while, but the winter is so cold, people weep over their chilblains and babies die from the cold and other babies die from inhaling smoke and coal dust and Samir says to me: We trade, we don't give.

Life with Mme. Colette, Famous Writer, Anti-Semite, Beloved Friend

Palais-Royal, Paris
1942

Mornings, I show up at the bakery, before school, for breakfast. Samir goes into the alley for his cigarette break—it astonishes me, Samir smoking, Samir working. Samir's pudgy belly, smooth as lambskin, hanging over his apron and out under his T-shirt, a cigarette in the corner of his mouth, like a grown man, and not a nice one. He brings me whatever goods have fallen onto the floor or been crushed in the morning rush. Sometimes he carries out a chipped demitasse and I take a sip of Turkish coffee and wrinkle my nose, like a baby, to show that I know that Samir is the head of the family now.

One morning Samir says: M. Lefond's hands are bothering him. He says: I told M. Lefond you're good at that, at the hand-rubbing.

I massaged my father's hands from the time I was six

until he died. He said it was a useful skill. He said: Some people have not even that to offer.

Samir takes me inside and we go right upstairs to the Lefond apartment. Mme. Lefond opens the door. She looks me over. She is reassured. I don't look like a husband-stealer or a Nazi spy, and someone has reassured her that despite the dark curls and the tilted eyes, I am not a Jew. Mme. Lefond goes downstairs to keep the croissants and brioches coming as long as they have the flour. Later in the day they make bread for the working people, and the dry dark loaves are so heavy, Samir says, that people have to shave them, not slice them.

M. Lefond, this is my sister, Gazala.

M. Lefond nods. He waves me closer.

He is a fatter, whiter version of my father. The big nose, the thin, still-black hair oiled to the scalp, the shuffle that tells me that his hips hurt and have hurt for the last twenty years and that beyond the hips are the bad knees and the swollen ankles and, above, a spine like an iron bar, and if all he needs is some hand-rubbing I'll be surprised. M. Lefond looks at me and I look at him. He sits in his armchair. I am so happy to be in a proper apartment, to breathe in the thick, eye-watering scent (I will learn that this is furniture polish—rancid lemon, ammonia, and walnut oil—and I love it), to sit on one of *several* chairs, to admire the dark wood table, with a *coffeepot* and a large cup (chipped, just like Samir's, and this pleases me too), and the faded green carpet—which is, nonetheless, *carpet*—stopping just short of the radiator, and even if the radiator is hissing very weakly there is carpet

and there is heat. I am not a husband-stealer, but if I could
be an apartment-stealer I would throw the Lefonds out and
keep house for me and Samir (and voilà, the actions of our
neighbor, the terrible Mme. Odette, are no longer a mystery
to me). The people who have what we want and cannot get
are worse than obstacles. They are enemies.

M. Lefond pushes his sleeves up on his arms. His arms
are like my father's, thick with silky black hairs and some
scattered gray hairs curling below the rough elbow. He rests
his hands on his knees. I bring my chair closer to him, and
then we both see that I would be bent in half like a bug to
work on his hands like that. So I sit on the floor and he
moves his feet and crosses his swollen ankles, gently.

I begin the way my father liked, a circle around the wrist
bones. I ask M. Lefond if they have any warm water to warm
up my fingers and he directs me to the coffeepot near the
stove. I wrap my hands around the coffeepot as long as I can.
The stove itself is cool. Around, around the wrists and down
the backs of his hands, avoiding the gray forked veins. (My
father didn't like his veins touched. Don't interfere, he said.) I
hear Mme. Lefond through the holes around the pipes chat-
ting up the customers. She is all sympathy and how hard
times are, so that no one will say about Lefond's: I see that the
fucking Germans get all the brioches and the buns.

Mme. Lefond says, sighing again: It's impossible to get
decent coffee. She says: My aunt mixes chicory and hot
water. Really, it's mostly a laxative. Some people boil acorns,
the man who works with Samir chimes in. (The Pole, Samir
calls him. I don't know his name.) I hear a woman say: Hon-

estly, we now drink herbal teas every night. You can find mint and lemon verbena in the parks.

Mme. Lefond says: Oh, you are so right. And it's impossible to get potatoes. My daughter needed to eat vegetables, so I gave her carrots until her hands turned orange. A customer laughs and says: My grandmother told me that when the Prussians surrounded the city during the last war, the best restaurants served Le chat flanqué de rats (Cat Flanked by Rats).

Everyone is hungry and everyone talks about food, stories of ingenuity or meals remembered (not everyone wants to hear about the simple, perfect chicken a woman we don't know made with rosemary and lemon and twenty-four cloves of garlic in 1939, but some customer wants to tell the story and stretches out her arms to show you just how big and fat the chicken was), or how people were making fools of themselves all over the city. Women collect these stories. At night, in the courtyard, a neighbor grabs me by my six-pocket coat and says: People are boiling rhubarb leaves like they're spinach. It's poison, she says, don't eat them. You have no one to tell you these things now. I know someone who ate a cat. Can you imagine? She picks up her filthy white cat and presses him to her cheek, like a witch in the fairy tales. His whiskers touch hers.

Mme. Lefond comes up the stairs, loudly, wearing the cork shoes all the women wear. (Not me. Samir has found me a pair of brown leather shoes with laces, and I care for them like jewels. When it rains, I carry them in my coat.) Mme. Lefond wears dark cork wedges, the uppers and straps dyed black. They do not flatter her. Her ankles, like her husband's, are giving out, like old chairs. Mme. Lefond takes off her shoes and I can see the design of the whole shoe on her dyed bare feet, black all the way to her toenails. She puts on her slippers and looks hard at M. Lefond. If he insists on sitting upstairs like a pasha, she will trudge downstairs like the martyr she is and wait on more people, despite her painful feet. She sighs. M. Lefond looks into the center of the room, blankly. No one looks at me.

Mme. Lefond goes back downstairs, sighing all the way, and I hear her revving up, encouraging the customers. A woman says that she nearly got run over by a big black car. She doesn't say "a German," but we all know who has the cars. Anyone who can manage a bit has a bicycle or shares one. Old people, young people. Mothers with one baby strapped in front and one in back. Businessmen. Teachers. The fashionable girls wear culottes so that their skirts don't get caught. Even the priests just shrug at that. A girl passed me one day and she'd tucked the back of her skirt into her sturdy serge underpants, and I saw other girls looking, thinking: That is not stupid. You cannot leave your bicycle unlocked, even if you take the wheels with you. Samir told me that a man stole his own brother's bicycle from in front of the bakery and his brother stabbed him with a bread knife. I long for a bicycle. I wonder, constantly, who might want to get me, or give me, a bicycle.

Downstairs, Mme. Lefond says, changing the subject from the Germans and their cars and all of France hiding like mice in front of the big black German cats: Maurice

Chevalier takes the Métro like everyone else does. I saw him, she says. Even Chevalier had to get off before curfew, she says. No one says anything.

I think that M. Lefond is pleased with the silence. I do each finger, joint by joint, and it's impossible not to be pleased by the successful cracking of every knuckle, each finger giving up its sharp exhalation. I can go up or down, at this point. Feet or shoulders. I am not going to rub this old man's feet for free, is what I think. But I would. I would rub his old feet and worse for his apartment, for a working stove, for a series of hot meals, for clean clothes for Samir and for me, and if you added hot water and a bath there is nothing I wouldn't do, and M. Lefond must feel my inclination, because he pats my hand, lightly, and cricks his neck to show what I should do next. I rub his neck and shoulders right up into the divot at the base of the skull, which used to make my father drop his chin to his chest and breathe through his mouth for a moment.

M. Lefond does the same.

Mme. Lefond comes back upstairs, quieter in her slippers, and she looks at me and her husband, his head dropped forward, and she waves her hand that I should go. I thought then that she resented me (what young girl does not believe that the basic stance of all old women is envy and fear?), but there were tears in her eyes and I think that she was worried that his work would kill her husband, like it did my father.

Before that happens, though, Mme. Lefond tells her friend who works at the fancy restaurant about the little Al- gérienne with the good hands who is doing so much good for poor Albert, and the friend she tells is old pals with Mme. Colette's housekeeper, and there is no one in Paris (meaning no one they know) who is not aware that Mme. Colette suffers the agonies of the damned with her arthritis and had even been to Switzerland to be injected with iodine in both hips and has had no results at all. Mme. Lefond walks me to Mme. Colette's house, and the housekeeper looks me up and down and says that I could pass for someone from the Midi, possibly Portuguese. I nod. She keeps her hand on my shoulder, brings me through to Madame's bedroom, and she offers me up to Mme. Colette like a canapé.

The bed itself is enormous, it is the size of a dining room table. It faces bookshelves, with many books, and there are more bookshelves behind the bed and also a few feathers, dried, dusty flowers, small clay pots, glass boxes of dead butterflies, their wings spread. The bed is lined up beside tall windows, and the room is still bright with morning light. There are four small chairs, in faded fabrics. And rugs upon rugs on the floor. Blankets upon blankets on the bed, and in the middle of the bed is Madame. I am small, and she is not smaller than me but also not a full-size white lady. Her hair is ridiculous, prostitute-orange flaming out in a big frizz, and her lips are carmine, the red seeping into the little lines around her mouth. Her eyes are slanted under the folds of her brows, kohl-rimmed cat's eyes in a dead-white face, powder in every fold and crack, and I can see that she is aware of all of it, of its effect, and she's pleased with it.

The housekeeper says: This is the girl I told you about. Good hands.

She gestures for me to hold up my unremarkable hands, and Madame beckons. I take one step and she waves me closer. I take another step and she beckons again, and finally, when I am a few inches away, she grabs me and pulls me to the bed so hard that my shins smack up against the wood frame. Thank you, Pauline, Madame says, and Mlle. Pauline goes out.

Magic hands, she says, amused. I say nothing. Mlle. Pauline has told me that if I am a success, there may be a room for me. There may be meals for me, and she said "meals," she did not say "a meal."

Do you speak?, Madame says.

I say: I do speak. And I see that Madame is listening very carefully, head cocked.

You are not Portuguese, she says.

I say nothing. I bring my hands up to my chest, just to remind her that these hands have been described as good, regardless of their origin. Where are you from?, she says.

I am from Paris, I say. Rue Caplat.

Well, she says in annoyance, I am from Paris now too, aren't I? Here we are, rue de Beaujolais. But I am from Saint-Sauveur-en-Puisaye in Burgundy. That is where I am from. If someone asked me, I would say I was a Burgundian.

And as she says it, she sounds less Parisian, more country, as I think of it.

I say: I am not a Burgundian. And her sharp yellow teeth gleam, and a little powder falls from her cheeks onto the wide collar of her green velvet jacket.

Madame waits.

My parents were Algerian, I say.

All right, she says. It's not so bad. I am part African, you know, and she turns her profile to me as if I will discern traces of Africa in her brow or her nose.

I am, she says. I used to love to dance, she says, as if this is also part of her Africanness. I was on stage, she says. Many years ago. She waves toward a photograph of a young woman with dark curls springing up under a headband with a big bow, a big necklace, a small waist and a big bottom, in an outfit that is some version of Egyptian.

I lower my hands and she bares her teeth, again.

You have a name, she says.

I do, I say.

Madame waits, tapping a finger on the bed frame.

I tell her my name.

She wins, no contest, fat, rich, and famous against skinny with cracked shoes, and we both know it, and then Mme. Colette relaxes, as most people do once they've bested you.

I am going to take off my bed jacket, she says. You are going to help me, she says, and then I would like you to massage my back and shoulders.

I help her off with the green jacket, and she is in a soft white nightshirt, yellowing at the neck, with a chemise under it. She sits up a bit more and twists to turn her back to me.

Madame, I say. I cannot. I can stand behind you as you sit in a chair or I can attend to you if you are lying down in your bed.

Neither of us can imagine me helping her to lie back in the bed, turn over, her face down in a pillow, with me astride her old back or leaning over her like I am washing the floor. She slides over to the edge of the bed and swings her legs toward the floor. She is no closer to planting her feet on the ground than I would be.

Madame, I say, I am going to pull the chair with the pink flowers very close to you and you will grab the arms and I will help you turn around. I do all this and she is a little out of breath, mostly from fear, I think, and her gown has ridden up to her ancient thighs, which have no flesh on them at all, pale, bruised sticks covered with little brown spots, thick and thin. I pull the gown down to cover everything and I pretend that I have not seen anything and she pretends that she has not seen me seeing and we are launched.

Do you have any oil?, I say.

Oil?

Face cream, some herbal oil. Some people have a little sandalwood oil or rosehip oil. Not cooking oil, unless you wish to smell like that, like a kitchen.

Duck fat at least, she says. I have face cream. Go into that armoire, there.

I open it and there are twenty jars of face cream, all with a label that says "Visage par Colette." I hold one jar up.

By all means, she says. I had a cosmetics empire, she says.

I take a scoop of the cream, thick as Camembert at the edges but not turned, I hope, and rub it between my hands.

Friends invested in my cosmetics empire, she says. Even the Galhai of Marrakesh—Thami El Glaoui. The Pasha.

Your people, she says. Beautiful man. Devoted. The business lasted a year. We lost every sou.

She pats my hand.

She says: One does what one must, wouldn't you say?

I nod, of course. She is my boss.

I cannot see you, she says. Speak up.

She is a very difficult woman.

So, of course: Yes, I say. One does. Yes.

I want the job and I get it, and Samir, who worries that I will be a cork in the ocean without his guidance, brings me the coat our father had made over for me, with food in every pocket and a Reichsmark. Samir says: I'll see you soon. He hugs me gently and says: Not soon, habibi.

I worry that just like with the Polish pâtissier and my father and with M. Lefond, I will never see Samir again.

I wash Madame's hair with a pitcher of water and a bowl to catch it. We are together, tranquil in her bedroom. Madame is in her big terrycloth robe. I scrunch up her curls until they are in the Colette pouf. We are waiting for Mme. Belperron, a jewelry designer.

The jewelry designer, Madame says. The only woman in a sea of men. Cartier is fine. Suzanne has audacity.

Madame says: Poor Suzanne. Dress me.

I dress her in her favorite green caftan and a shawl and another shawl over her legs.

Mme. Belperron arrives with a gift, one of her own jewelry designs, which is wise. She sits down and brings out a lady's pin wrapped in tissue paper. Wrinkled white tissue paper, not fresh. Blue ribbon. Green stones tucked inside gold wire. Mme. Belperron lays the gift on the side table and demonstrates how it comes apart, and she shows us, hands in the air, that the large pin can be separated into a pair of ear clips shaped like sparkling flowers. It is the prettiest and cleverest thing I have ever seen.

Mme. Belperron glances at me for the first time. She smiles.

"This was for the Duchess of Windsor," she says. "But."

"Very, very clever," Madame says. "And beautiful. And surprising. It is exceptional, Suzanne. Thank you. It has been too long," Madame adds, and if you didn't know her, you would think that she'd been longing, day and night, for a visit from Suzanne Belperron and not cursing me all morning as if the visit was my fault.

Mme. B. reads aloud a bit from her letter to the Duchess of Windsor, and Madame makes little noises of appreciation. The letter is good and very polite, and as hard as I am and as hard as Mme. B. makes herself, I want to cry. Mme. B. lets the Duchess of Windsor know that M. Bernard Herz, whom Mme. B. loves even more than she loves her own husband (as Madame has explained to me), is being held at an internment camp near Compiègne for the crime of being a Jew. She says this, in the letter, without using the words "camp," "crime," or "Jew." She shows us a small sketch in the letter's lower right corner, and I understand, and Madame understands, and I am sure even the Duchess (a cow and a Nazi,

Madame says) understands, that were M. Herz to find his way home in the next week, a gold bracelet with a double row of cabochon amethysts would find its way to the Duchess very soon. Madame looks at me to make tea.

"I have written another letter," Mme. B. says. "In this one I wrote: 'As you may know, M. Bernard Herz is the supplier for all of our pearls and precious stones. He has been picked up, most unfortunately, through what is undoubtedly a misunderstanding. M. Bernard Herz served France heroically while in the military as a young man. My husband—' See, that was the touch I needed, to show that Jean and I, we love M. Herz but it is not, actually, *personal*."

Mme. B. sounds like she will vomit.

Mme. B. keeps reading. "'My husband and I wish nothing more than to see to the release of M. Herz as he is a Frenchman, a citizen of the world, and, of course, a great supporter of the arts, most especially in the world of jewelry, and without him I would not have been able to create for you and the Duke in the last few years. Yours most sincerely, Suzanne Belperron.'"

She shows us her bold, clean signature, which takes up a good quarter of a page. She shows us a second page, a small sketch, yellow squiggles and green ovals. Underneath, in her handwriting: *gold and tourmalines*.

Mme. B. picks up Madame's obsidian lighter, shaped like a turban, and lights the letter on fire.

"I did finally hear from her, two weeks ago. She must have figured that either Bernard was free, and I would be in a good mood, or he was dead, and I would be desperate for

work. A good guess, right? I suppose I am sharing the letters
with you because who else in this world can tell me how to
write an even better letter and save Bernard?"

Madame shakes off a couple of shawls like an old war-
horse hearing the bells of battle. She lifts her head. If you
need a superb, persuasive letter to gain the release of your
diamond merchant lover, why not turn to Mme. Colette. To
whom else? As Madame says to me later: Well, let's be frank,
whom should you ask? Proust? Pas possible. Cocteau?

Madame smiles, and Mme. B. looks a little hopeful.

Suzanne Belperron joins us for roast chicken and
creamed cauliflower and some heavy rye bread. I take my
tray to the corner and I eat everything. I eat everything,
every day. I hear Mme. B. say that she is delighted, that Madame is too kind. Madame says, as she always does, that her
little farmers, her little angels of the countryside, are looking
after her. Sometimes she lists, to me, what they send her,
practically singing about the radishes, the fresh eggs, the
brussels sprouts, but she holds back today. (We talk about
food all the time. Paris is the capital of hunger but not for
Madame and not for her friends. When Madame offered me
room and board I thanked her, and now I sit in the tiny
room she has set aside for me and I scream into my coat for
sheer joy.)

Mme. B. says, "Do you know, I even wrote to Chanel. I
sent a charming little pin—one I had, not my design, a pearl
on a stick, nothing like this one I brought to you—and I sent
a note by courier, right to the Ritz. We know a lot of the
same people. As we do. People photograph my jewels on

Chanel's jackets, don't they? I thought: Why not? At the beginning of the war, she'd shut her business. She said, in public, it was not a time for fashion. It was not a time to pay her
workers a living wage, I can tell you that. I think she hated
every woman who ever worked for her. I think she hates all
women."

Madame makes a faint face of protest. Coco Chanel is
famous for telling everyone that Colette is her favorite writer.
Madame does say, "She certainly hates the Jews, she never
shuts up about it. She tried to get the Nazis to protect her
business, but she couldn't quite. Those Wertheimer boys
outsmarted her, even there. And I am quite a fan of the
younger Wertheimer."

Madame says nothing about M. Maurice, her Jewish
husband who is, right now, reading an old magazine and
eating soup, with his shoes off, while sitting on my bed in the
attic. We share a room very often, and he is the soul of po-
liteness and never lets me sleep on the floor. They love each
other so much. They both tell me so, and even if they did
not, I have eyes. She is the Queen, he is the Prince. She is the
genius, and he is the man who supports the genius, and
when anyone raises an eyebrow and says: But she's seventeen years older than you, but she must outweigh you by
twenty kilos, also you were a nothing, a minor pearl merchant with a wealthy father and the perfect extra man at any
dinner party, he laughs and puts his hand over his heart and
says: What a beautiful thing, to be rescued by Colette, and
he means it, and no one laughs after that. When the Germans take him to Compiègne, where they take the Jews be-

fore they send them to die in Germany, Madame does not
talk to anyone about the shit she has to eat to get him out.
(She dines with the German ambassador's wife and tells me,
when she comes home, that the food was German but there
was lots of it, and she'd written an awful novel that the Germans praised, and I like to think it was written just to curry
favor.) When I read the novel, *Julie de Carneilhan* (it is a joke
between us that her little maid likes to read, but it is true, and
she is flattered by my interest and I am flattered to be seen as
a voracious reader, which I am not; human beings are more
than enough for me), even I who do not always perceive nu-
ance on the page can see that the man is a grasping homo-
sexual and the rich widow is a terrible Jewish spider, in too
many diamonds, reeking of too many perfumes. I told Madame that I was reading *Julie*, and she said to me, in a rare
tone: You needn't, girl.

Maybe it is Madame's ferocity and cleverness and the
German ambassador's wife's admiration and Madame's terrible novel that brings M. Maurice home months later, ten
kilos lighter (reclaiming my boyish figure, he says). When he
comes home, Madame is undone. She does not quake in the
face of trouble, her approach is to rise above it, to focus on
the meal or the work or the animals, but relief breaks her.
She sleeps for days. When she recovers, they celebrate, quietly but at every occasion, even when they buy her first
wheelchair and even when the Germans get serious. The
Jews wear the yellow stars, including M. Maurice (no reason
not to, Madame said, and M. Maurice said nothing), and
then in July there was no more pretend. So many Jews—

every Jew I knew or had met or heard of—were sent away. Thousands and thousands.

M. Maurice goes away for a few months, to the south, hoping to be safer there, and then he felt—he tells me—that Madame could not bear the worry and Madame agreed and he came back to Paris.

Madame says to me: M. Maurice will not be, officially, at home. We do not discuss, with other people, how many people live in our house, how many meals are prepared. We avoid unpleasantness.

I nod. I also dislike unpleasantness. And busybodies.

M. Maurice needs to be invisible, from evening until breakfast, Madame says. He will spend that time in your room.

With me?, I say.

Madame does not answer.

I know. I can sleep in the tub. I can sleep in the street. She loves me, in her way, but M. Maurice is her life, and without Madame, I would have been fucking German soldiers for potatoes. I am happy to share my room.

M. Maurice hides for eighteen months, in our attic room, from nightfall to breakfast time, and we all hope that this is, if not safe, safer than M. Maurice wandering around the south of France, with his charming smile, counting on good luck.

The next time Mme. Suzanne Belperron visits, she has something more to say about Chanel. "Not even von Dincklage—

Chanel loves the 'von'; you know, her mother did laundry, her father was a bum—not even von Dincklage can make it all right for her. What a cow. I'm sure she won't write back."

Madame says, "I have three suits from her and I have one evening gown and I don't own anything more chic and I do not wear them. I never do." She gestures to her robes and shawls and the velvet blanket over her legs. "It's not entirely an act of virtue, of course."

Afterward, Madame says: Once in a while, I'd like you to go there. Bring Mme. Belperron some eggs. If she doesn't have anyone to wash the dishes, wash the dishes.

Mme. Belperron does not send for me, and I do not volunteer. A month later, we get a note from Mme. B., big as a menu, her handwriting wild, dark blue up and down the page: *Colette, Bernard is returned. If you had anything to do with this, thank you. And if not, please know that my visits to you have been a great comfort. I will see you soon. With great affection, Suzanne B.*

Now you go to her, Madame says. Be useful.

The Price of Life Is Grief

Montmartre, Paris
1942

I am cleaning, in the Belperron bathroom, on my knees, on the bathmat and a pile of towels. It's too hard on my knees otherwise. There is something wrong with my knees. They have knobs of bone, like buttons, sticking out below my kneecaps. Samir said that if I ever weigh enough, the buttons will disappear. You'll be smooth, he said.

M. Bernard Herz is having tea and reading the paper, and it's as if the terrible thing hadn't happened, as if he hadn't been in Compiègne for three months while Mme. B. cried and worked and dragged herself to Madame's apartment to gossip and express her feelings and eat lunch.

M. Bernard Herz looks old and thin. Mme. B. had told me that M. Herz had not looked well when he came home from Compiègne and he has not really gained back the weight.

———

I served at lunch two days ago, on loan again from Madame.
(Mme. B. worries that the French girls will make some issue
over M. Herz or the black market pork or something, and I
cannot tell her she is wrong. But I can serve from the left,
take from the right, hang up a fur coat and a silk scarf without dropping or stealing either, and my plans do not include
denunciations of elderly Jews or their mistresses.)

Their guests are another couple, a goldsmith and his
quiet wife. They talk about food, as everyone does, and news
of their children—the goldsmith's sons are prisoners of
war—so there is just a little quiet crying and the men pour
some wine and clear their throats.

Bernard Herz is a good man. He clasps the goldsmith's
hands and says that they will keep working together, that
the goldsmith is a genius with metal and that his lovely wife
is the real jewel. The four of them clink glasses. The goldsmith begins a sentence: After the war . . . And they all inhale sharply, but M. Herz exhales and makes a big gesture,
opening his arms. Wars end, he says, which is a safe way to
put it. I can see that the goldsmith and his wife are glad to
see M. Herz again, that they love him, in fact, in that quiet
country way, and they admire Mme. B. for the original she
is. Who else runs a big business, is in all the fashion magazines, creates jewelry to astonish the world, devotes herself
publicly and privately to an old Jew, and keeps her own husband, Jean, in line and not unhappy twenty miles away?

After the guests go home, Mme. B. rises from the table.
She stops smiling. M. Herz sits in his armchair and takes off
his glasses. Mme. B. looks at me, and I bring M. Herz a glass

of mineral water. I put it on the malachite table. M. Herz says: In the next few weeks we have to pick up the reins of the business. He says to Mme. B.: I need to finish that paperwork, this needs to be your business entirely. Aryanization, my dear. Belperron Jewelry.

Mme. B. shuffles a deck of cards. (She plays Fascination in the afternoons.)

I know, she says.

M. Herz says: What would you have me do?

Mme. B. shrugs.

My dear, he says, I could just leave it to my barber, he's not a Jew.

Not that we know, Mme. B. says, and M. Herz does smile a little. He is afraid to go to the office but he makes himself go, every Monday, for a couple of hours, and finally today she says to him: Stop going. I'm signing, she says. I'll sign everything.

Please come tomorrow, Mme. B. says to me.

I do go back. I hang up my shawl (Madame's old green shawl) and walk into the kitchen. I wipe my hands. M. Herz shakes his head no. He doesn't need anything, and he would like me to finish cleaning the bathroom and go. He is never unkind or rude, he is polite and he is half-dead when Mme. B. is not around. The man is cooped up in Mme. B.'s apartment, his boy is a prisoner of war, his wife, a decent woman, is dead, and his mistress runs and now owns his business, making good and bad decisions about his life's work, to which he will probably never return. I hear him folding the newspaper and putting his plate into the sink.

M. Herz doesn't allow himself to say anything about all the lies in the newspaper, or about the Germans, or about Maréchal Pétain, ever.

I am straddling the bidet, whose purpose I now understand but whose nozzles and sprays still surprise me, when I hear four hard knocks on the front door. Onetwothree and— *four.* More knocks, by a heavier hand. I push the bathroom door closed. I roll up the bathmat and push it up against the door sill.

I hear French voices, and there is a German one too. It is always worse when the Germans come. They do not yell, but they are raising their voices, to hurry M. Herz, to frighten him. I can hear that M. Herz does not go into the desk where he keeps all their papers. Every drawer in the speckled maple desk has letters and papers and sketches of Mme. B.'s beautiful jewelry. There is a leather folder with the important papers in it: baptism certificates and wedding photographs—his and hers—and wedding certificates—his and hers—and the birth certificate of his son, Jean, and Jean's official papers from the French Army. There is the death certificate of M. Herz's late wife, Mme. Jeanne, whom I never met, who seemed to have had a quiet life and death in some pleasant town and perhaps did not mind about Mme. B., who is all glamour and silk and red fingertips even now. I read all those papers while Mme. B. was out, one day, while M. Herz was in Compiègne, because you never know. I think that M. Herz should grab the papers to show them something, something in his favor, and then I think that he should not.

It will not help this time, I could tell from the knocks,

and there is no one who will not be hurt by the connection to M. Herz. Mme. B. told me one night that Rika Radifé helped get M. Herz out of Compiègne the first time. She said: I can't ask Rika again. Not that Rika would help. Rika's become Catholic. She is a flagrant Catholic now, more Catholic than the Pope. Our Lady of the Vatican. Poor Rika and her poor husband, they looked like Jews, so they had to make the extra effort, what can you do? Mme. B. crunched up her smooth dark hair with both hands to make what she thinks are wild Jewish curls.

M. Herz opens the door. A Frenchman asks M. Herz if he is alone. He says: Oh, yes, I am alone. They say: Where is your wife?, and he says: My wife is dead. One of the Frenchmen says, very rudely: We know where your mistress is, we are arresting her right now. M. Herz says nothing. M. Herz does not take his papers. I hear him open the front hall closet and I picture him getting his hat and his coat. His gray gloves are in the left pocket and I hope that he brings his challis scarf and I grab my own ears so that I can hear and not hear, until all the men have walked out. They do not shut the front door. I stay in the bathroom until nighttime.

Mme. B. comes home at eight. It is dark in the apartment and dark outside. I hear her heels across the floor. (Mme. B. has kept her high heels. You will not see her in wooden clogs or cork shoes unless the world has ended.) She turns on the front hall light. I open the bathroom door and call out to her: Madame, Madame, it's Gazala. I am here. I don't want to frighten her. I don't want her to kill me by accident. I have heard of this happening, people being mistaken for burglars, or being burglars, and being brained with a lamp by a fed-up homeowner. I walk into the hall and she is standing there, still in her coat. She sits down on the couch and gestures that I should come over. I don't want to sit on the couch. My clothes are grimy and damp with sweat.

"What happened?" she says.

I tell her what I heard from my place in the bathroom.

"Oh, sit," she says. "You know, the first time they took M. Herz, December, last year, when they brought me in for interrogation, the Germans sat in the front of the car. Because I am a lady and not a Jew, they let me sit in the back-seat. I am in my fur coat. In my fur coat."

She says that she had managed not to cry then. One of the Germans kept saying: Mme. Belperron, what is this Jew-ish man to you? And she says that she told him: Herz is my business partner. And a great friend to me and my husband. And, she says to me, that is the moment when she is so glad that she married Jean Belperron. Because the reason for that marriage, she sees now, is so that she might protect Bernard Herz.

Love is a funny thing, she says. You know, you work for Madame. Mme. B. reads me the notes she has made for her husband's letter to the German officer. She reads me an-other early draft of one of her many letters to the Duchess of Windsor: Monsieur Herz, the supplier for all of our pearls and precious stones, as you know, has been picked up, most unfortunately, blah blah blah. My husband and I wish nothing more than to see to his release as he is a Frenchman, a citizen of the world, blah blah.

In the dark, with her shoes off, Mme. Belperron recites the list of all the food she'd sent M. Herz before, when he was in Compiègne: canned peaches, cured ham, dried fruit, things like that.

He was gone for three and a half months that time, she says. They put them all in the École Militaire and then they took them to Royallieu, near Compiègne. I was charming, she says. I negotiated and negotiated, and what is that, really? I begged. One pig said to me that it seemed as if I was in love with him, and I said: Oh, la, if you knew him, you would love him too, he is a dear little man.

And then he was home and we picked up, we tried to pick up, the reins of business, as he says. M. Herz is a sensible man. We just finished all that paperwork to turn the business over to me entirely. I signed today.

She looks at me.

"How old are you?"

I lie about my age constantly, but I cannot see that it matters here much whether I am twelve or sixteen or the more worrying eighteen.

"I am just fourteen," I say, hedging.

"Well, I apologize. The things one finds funny, at the edge of the abyss, even in the abyss, they are not funny to young people. Bernard, M. Herz, needed to go in to the office, but he was afraid. Not that he said so. He made himself go. And then, after a few days, he came home and he stayed home. He said that it was better not to call attention to himself. And then he proposed."

I sit still and I don't say: But, Mme. Belperron, what about M. Belperron?

"He said that however long he had, before the Germans came back, he wanted to be with me. We are French"—unlike you—"and we accommodate. Obviously."

She gestures outside.

"The Nazis came in and we did nothing. They killed our citizens, they are filthy murderers, and our great protest is to have Piaf singing for the German troops while telling ourselves that this is somehow not collaboration. Disgusting. My country is disgusting."

Mme. B. gets up, still in the dark, and pours herself a brandy. She offers me one and I say yes, because no one has ever offered me a brandy. I drank something yellow from one of Madame's cut glass decanters a few weeks ago and had to spit it into the kitchen sink.

Mme. B. tells me, "When M. Herz was picked up the first time, I called everyone I knew, and when I called my *husband* I said, 'My dear Jean, terrible news. Bernard, yes, *our* Bernard, has been picked up by the police.' (I said 'police,' to make it sound . . . less Jewish.) 'What a mess, what a misunderstanding. I know you have some friends,' I said. Jean's brother is a pig, a police captain, and I thought: My brother-in-law must have friends. He wasn't one of those who took early retirement when the Germans came. On the contrary. I say to Jean, 'Do you think your brother might make a call,

just to see if we can get this sorted out?' Do you know what
my husband, Jean Belperron, said, and why I was so glad,
right then, that I had married him? He said, 'Terrible thing.
I will call Pierre, my dear.' And later he said that he did ask
Pierre and his brother said he had no intention of sticking
his fat neck out to help the Jewish friend of his brother's
oddball wife. I, however—"

She takes off her dress and drops it onto the floor. She
sits up, in her underwear. One of her silk stockings snags on
the wooden corner of the couch. She reaches down her leg
and sticks her finger into the hole, furiously pulling it down
to her ankle, like smashing a plate.

"I, however, I wrote to the Duchess of Windsor." She
smiles. "Again."

She gets up, and I see her as she is, besides all the glamour she carries (Madame says that glamour is useful but it
does not take the place of style), a middle-aged woman,
square-shouldered and sturdy in her slip and underclothes
and the torn stocking, and she throws things out of her desk
drawer onto the floor. She throws pads of paper and colored
pencils and there are a few pieces of colored chalk, for her
drawings, and they land on the white rug. I see that she sees
what she has done and that I am not to move.

"Here it is," she says. "Here's the sketch. Very nice, no?
You see? You remember?"

It is better than nice. It pulses with color on the page,
and I am taken with the idea of a person making this thing,
making it with little hammers and little torches, with calipers
and tweezers. My father could have done that, my brother

could have done that, and I think that I could do it too, our clever hands.

Madame had told me, in private, that the Duchess of Windsor was a horse-faced cunt and a Nazi lickspittle and will no more help M. Bernard Herz than she will set herself on fire.

Mme. B. puts a silk pillow under her head and tells me the whole story of M. Herz and Compiègne, again. The letter, the sketches, the cleverness, the cured ham she was able to get to M. Herz. I want to get back to the happy ending, to M. Herz at the breakfast table every morning, pursing his lips a little over the chicory coffee and Mme. B. smiling, saying once—only once—that it is a little bit funny that with all that is happening outside their door, he, M. Herz, can still find it in himself to be disappointed—every morning—by weak coffee. M. Herz makes it clear that he will not complain again and that there is nothing funny in her remarks.

Mme. Belperron says to me, "I wrote to my husband, M. Belperron, again two weeks ago, and then I went to see him at our house, my Belperron house. I told my Jean I needed to be with Bernard as long as possible. Jean was very kind. If you marry," she says to me, "you should marry someone with whom it would be possible to be friends. And so the business papers were all signed. And perhaps the Germans were waiting for that, for all the ribbons to be tied up, and now they have come for him. Again."

She comes over to me and opens an envelope.

"See this?" she says. "In order to make jewelry now, you have to buy your own metal. So . . ."

She slides into my hand a bit of wood with a stone in it.

"That's the prototype," she says. "I'll put a diamond in a piece of narrow driftwood and attach a strong clasp, and voilà, my sand and stone collection. You keep this one."

I take it and later I sell it. A mistake.

I sleep on Mme. Belperron's couch, and when the sun comes up we both wake up, and from across the room she tells me more things.

"Really, the first time M. Herz was taken did not go so badly for me, because I am a lady—that is to say, I am not a whore or a concierge and my father was a respectable merchant, but that's a far cry from being a lady—and because I was wearing a filigreed gold cross, the biggest one I could find, and, absolutely, because every newspaper in Europe carried a photograph of the Führer kissing the Duchess's hand at Berchtesgaden while the Duke beamed, and everyone could see, right above that hand, the bracelet I designed for the Duchess's knobby wrist. And so they let me sit in the backseat, that time.

"I opened my round alligator-skin handbag, you know the one, with the amber-and-alligator clasp, I found my little green silk address book, and I began to eat the pages. Discreetly, in the backseat. It was impossible to see which page was which in the dark of the car, so I had to begin toward the end, where the Jewish names might be. Milhaud, Naquet, Stryzma, Weil. You know what I mean," she says, "not the Belfonds, the Belmonts, the Belperrons. I tore each page

into two strips by rolling them up and down, and then I
chewed and swallowed very quietly until we got to the interrogation. The German officer took my hand to help me out
of the car.

"I didn't cry," she says. "I would not cry. Also, they were
still being polite. They were still pretending that Paris would
be Germany's holiday city. They would be the owners and
we would be the poodles, but we would at least be poodles,
not . . . not . . ."

Neither of us knows what is beneath poodles. I want to
say that it would be worse to be a rat, but my impression of
many of the French people I meet is that they *are* rats, scrap-
ing for crumbs, hiding in the corners, showing their teeth to
the smaller rodents and diving into the filth when the bigger
creatures come. Let us not be worse than rats, I think.

Mme. B. waves her hand for some tea, and she waves
that I should have some tea, too. The lights are still off.

"The German officer spoke French that time. Of course
he spoke French, I don't speak German. He says to me, 'Madame, what is this man, this Herz, to you?' I say, 'He is a
great businessman,' and then I see I must rethink this. They
think all Jews are great businessmen, they will think he is an
international banker, they will think he's like that show
they're having in the Palais Berlitz. Did you see it?"

I did see it. Half of Paris saw it. *Le Juif et la France*. It ran
for weeks and tickets were cheap. They set up loudspeakers
at the corners blaring shitty French songs about the French
countryside. The announcer begins very dignified, telling
people that they, and they alone, can save France by educat-

ing themselves about the insidious Jewish criminals, but by
the end the voice is just screaming: *Save France! Save France!*
Inside, they had posters of actual French Jews, all men. There
was a big picture of M. Wolff Lévitan, who had owned the
Lévitan store on rue du Faubourg Saint-Martin, which I had
loved wandering through in my little-girl pinafore with the
big pockets and, again, my clever hands. The Nazis had liq-
uidated it in July 1941, and they sold everything inside to
Germans. In '43, they made it into a showcase for all the
goods they'd stolen from the Jews. Every sofa was cleaned,
every brass fitting polished. You could get plates, bowls,
mugs, shaving sets. I heard you could walk down the middle
corridor, past room after room of furniture, each arranged
as if maman and papa would soon be sitting down to dinner, or listening to the radio, or pulling up the embroidered
counterpane on their four-poster mahogany bed. I think
they made Jewish prisoners work there. I wanted to walk
through one time to see if what people said could possibly
be true, but whatever I look like, I don't look German, and I
don't have the clothes to look like an Offiziere Matratze, an
officer's mattress.

Mme. B. stands up and looks out the window, into the
morning, and she lies back down on the couch. "It was different last night. This time, they still let me sit in the back of
the car, by myself, with my coat on, and when we get to
headquarters I say that M. Herz was my business partner—
before we Aryanized the company, of course. I emphasize
that it is now Suzanne Belperron SARL and that M. Herz
had been a great friend to my husband, Jean, and myself.

When they came to the subject of the visit, I brought out my wedding picture to show them that Jean and I are a real Catholic couple, that there is nothing fishy going on, and also there are a dozen crosses everywhere in the photo, around my neck, behind us, over the church door. My mother loved the church we got married in. Saint-Siméon."

She says the name of their little church, in which I'm sure Mme. Belperron has not been for twenty years, and her eyes fill with tears and I know that she is glad that her mother is not here to see all of this.

"The German looks at the wedding photo and he hands it back to me. He says that Jean Belperron and I must be very fond of my Jew, to have sent him packages and pressed my case with them last time. I see that I have guessed wrong again. I should have spoken of M. Herz with contempt, to make it sound as if it was always the business I cared about, not the man, but it's too late. The German officer stands up and says, 'Thank you, Madame,' and I was driven home by a regular soldier, not an officer, and I do not know what that means."

I don't move toward her. With Madame, I take the shoes and clean them and drag her poor old self into her big bed and sometimes hold her hand, but that is not who Mme. B. is to me. She is the friend, of sorts, of my Madame, and I am her borrowed girl. I don't think we owe each other very much.

She gets up, still in her coat, and her shoes leave mud at the end of the ivory sofa. I stay until her head falls back onto the cushion and then I move the teacup and saucer to the malachite table, which matches her lighter. I put on my wrap (Madame's wrap), and my hand is on the doorknob when Mme. B. says: Yesterday, M. Herz proposed to me. I said yes.

She says: I wanted someone to know.

Mint Tea

Palais-Royal, Paris
1944

Mme. Colette waits for the journalist to ask more questions.
This girl has come to interview Madame, and for five minutes she has been quoting Madame to Madame on the subject of their shared rapture over the wildness of pure nature
and romantic love. Madame begins to fall asleep. I will not
let her, will not let her be embarrassed. I dig my hands into
Madame's thin, soft old skin, the poor twists of muscle no
more than dough underneath. I whisper that Madame
should wake up, that I might tear her skin with all the knead-
ing. Madame straightens her neck and snorts. She whispers:
If this girl keeps talking, you may tear me apart until there's
nothing left.

Your genius, the girl taking notes says, what is the source
of your genius?

Madame and I look at each other.

Some mint tea?, Madame asks the girl, who's dressed
exactly the way Madame tells French girls not to: the tower-

ing hat, a foot higher than her little head, with folds every few inches, covered in rosettes of tightly curled thick ribbon, to look like a rosebush of green roses, and her dress as thin and short as a chemise, halfway up her skinny thighs, and of course the cork wedges. Hers are dark blue, probably stained with ink, and I can see the blue streaks, dark to light, over her pale ankle bones.

Mint tea, Madame, I say.

It's my Josephine Baker moment, performing North African Girl with Teapot. *Thé vert à la menthe, atay bil naânaâ,* Madame says in her awful Burgundian Arabic. When Madame hears real Algerians speak French, she gets a very kind look on her face. That is the face I show her now. Very kind. I make a proper fuss with the pale green tea, pouring it back and forth between the glass and the pretty silver teapot, like my mother's but bigger and brighter, of course. (Tooth powder, Madame has said, you just brush it with tooth powder and an old toothbrush and rinse with warm water. As if that will make the teapots alike.) I add honey to the tea with a free hand, more honey than anyone has seen in Paris that last year, because Madame has her ways and although even Madame cannot get sugar and that's just the way it is, she can get honey.

Mint. I've grown herbs outside Madame's big windows, on the sliver of windowsill. Mint, thyme, and lavender, which is as south of Paris as we can get now, with Madame's painful hips and poor M. Maurice upstairs in my little closet, hiding from the Germans. I stuff the teapot with handfuls of mint leaves and do the Maghrebi show of shows, pouring the tea from high above my shoulder down into the pretty glasses.

Keesan, Madame says, that's what they call the glasses. I make the kind face. The girl nods. Her stupid turban bobs and slips forward a bit.

Madame says: Of course it was the British who brought it to North Africa. A British merchant, because of the Crimean War, his ship was stuck, and he had much too much and sold his tea in the Mediterranean. The Maghrebi (and again she sounds like an old drunk) improved it, of course, waving her hand again in appreciation of my people and our clever ways and, perhaps, some wry amusement at how little it has gotten us.

Maghreb means sunshine, Madame says, and puts out her hand for the glass, looking right into my eyes, like we are conspiring girls. *Let's wrap this party up* is the message. I do one last waterfall pour and the French girl gasps a little bit and I do not spill a drop.

Ragwa style, Madame says, and I look at her, thinking, *You* wrap it up, Madame, it is your party. Madame looks out the big window, toasting the sky with her red glass.

A good storyteller gives you the gray great mountains around Oran, the red flowers and orange brush of the desert. The pine forests. The dark blue sweep of the water. The great bronze lions of Oran. (Algerian people used to say "I am as brave as the Lions of Oran," my father told me, and Samir would wave his hand like a paw.) The good storyteller brings you to the side of the main road as villagers carry white-wrapped corpses up the left side for the Muslim cemetery, down the right for the Christian. A good storyteller has memories and caraway seeds and cinnamon sticks and candied dates in his pocket, like an old uncle. My father was not, as these things go, a good storyteller. Madame is a great storyteller. Great on the page and even better in the room, no difference between the lie and the wish.

The first glass is as gentle as life,
the second glass is as strong as love,
the third glass is as bitter as death.
There is no Maghrebi who doesn't know this.

Schöner Mann

Parc des Buttes-Chaumont, Paris
1944

In Paris, we have another terrible winter. The sun is having
a moment, as high and bright as the winter sun gets. The
clouds have a thin, nearly pink edge. The plane trees are in
the same sad shape as the winter before and the winter before that: branches bent and broken from the weight of the
ice and by people in icy rooms burning the branches in their
wastebaskets or stoves or under a bridge on a dry stone. The
Russians and Poles who are still around say it looks just like
home. Parisians used to have prettier women and better
food, but this winter if you are French and look good you are
probably a Nazi or a collabo, and our winters are now as
cold as Poland's. I am sixteen.

The pink passes, and streams of bluish light drown in
the park shadows. Some big bushes still hold their leaves.
Without the bushes, there'd be no kissing, no *schmusen*.
There'd be no place come dusk for me to lie beneath the
German (*Schöner Mann*, I said. Handsome man.) and unbut-

ton his jacket at the neck. I roll to the side. He is concerned. Have I changed my mind?

I put my finger to my mouth and smile. I ask him if I can sit on top of him. Tiny little me, great hulking him. Master of the universe and adorable piece of garbage. He smiles. He waves his hand in welcome and I climb on, giggling, as if I have only just now, under the influence of his charm and good looks, realized that this new pleasure could be mine. I sit squarely on him. I unbutton his tunic to the middle of his chest. I squirm over his belt. (Those buttons, I say. That belt!) My right hand is still on my tattered handbag, a gift from Madame after most of the embroidery has worn off. The brown leather is intact and the clasp still works. The whole unimpressive thing is the length of a breakfast baguette. Or a bread knife. I unbutton another button. It's coming in dusk properly now, the best time for ambiguous actions. Am I reaching for my handbag (a handkerchief? a barrette for my wild hair?) or am I just scrabbling at the dead leaves in a spurt of startling, surprising desire? Is that the click of the clasp or the slide of my heavy knickers under my short-for-rationing skirt?

Who can say? Not this Fritz.

I narrate every moment this way, to myself. I am tough. I am Jean Gabin, the toughest tough guy, down by the pier, smoking a hand-rolled cigarette, contemplating my next move. I am, in these moments, as hard as I know how to be.

I find the handle. I put my left hand on his left shoulder to arc him up a little bit, and I wish he would scowl at my brass, like the first one did, or look away, lips pursed in disapproval, like the second. This one smiles, warmly, like a lover. Like a lucky young man who's found a pretty local girl, innocent but game, foolish but not a fool. If I want him lifted up, closer to me, if I want to feel him more through his trousers, to let him begin to ease those trousers down, he is happy to arc.

He's not a big man, none of that appealing German heartiness. Bratwurst. Bockwurst. French women and French queers love the look of the soldiers. Everyone's longing for fucking and food, and there they are, two for one. I am careful not to pick the stallions, who would break me in half, but my first two were muscled and pink. This one is still pale after a hot summer, with a thin neck under his uniform and a few pimples at the edge of his haircut. He has a big sunburned nose, and he frowns when I pull back. He grabs me by the waist, hard. His smile is gone and he says: *Hure.* I am returned to myself. I am ashamed that I hesitated.

I look right up his nose as I make myself smaller and curl back, pulling my stomach in so that I am resting entirely on my heels, and I rock a few times. I push the knife, three times, as fast and hard as I can, into his liver. I don't have the strength for his chest or his neck.

He inhales deeply, gasping, and I roll off him and crouch in a running position. If he gets up to hurt me, I can run faster than he can, for a bit, and I have left my borrowed bicycle at the other entrance to the park. I'll be gone before he knows it.

You've done this before is what I'm thinking. Talk talk talk, walk walk walk, boom boom boom. I know what I'm doing. I think it in rhythm with my heartbeat. Done this, know that, done this, know that. If he doesn't get up, I'll go around him and stab him twice more right beneath his undershirt, be-

neath the white ribs of his skinny chest. He is blinking many
times, and he looks at me as if I will save him, as if whoever
has done this terrible thing is gone and there is only me, who
might thrust my sweater into the wound, stanch the blood,
lift his head, call for help. I watch him twitching on the
ground, groaning softly, his bony white fingers tapping
among the leaves. I cry and I walk quickly to my bike. I do
not run. I do everything right: both hands on the handle-
bars, both feet on the pedals, single file, and I do not even
think of grabbing the back of a truck for a free ride.

Everyone behaves themselves while we wait for the war to
end. The yellow stars mocking the Germans with witty phrases
(*Zazou! Swing!*), the whistling when we ride bikes past the German troops, the boys with their splashy ties or two oars (*deux
gaules,* you see) over the shoulder, it all dries to a trickle. The
Germans change their tactics, and if you are willing to die for
Free France you know that painting graffiti and whistling aren't
enough to make a difference but are absolutely enough to get
you killed. People my age stop demonstrating. The few, the
extraordinary, are reckless and quiet, carrying messages, trans-
porting parts and maps and necessary copper wire in the back
of a boot or the cup of a brassiere. If I were a proper criminal
I would have thrown the knife into the river, but it is our best
bread knife and I am not careless with Madame's things.

I am not careless.

They parade women down the street into the town
squares, they shave the girls' heads and rip off their clothes:
the nineteen-year-old widow who saw a little of her poor
late husband in the boy billeted nearby, the woman running

the farm with no one but her grandfather and the German officer who was polite and spoke French, the whore who was asked by the mayor to service Germans and did. These women, who betrayed no one worse than their own selves, are the symbol of French shame, and the French men and their women kick those girls like dogs, and after kicking the girls like dogs go on home and are ashamed, and the rest of the French, like all men, are relieved and pleased, only a little ashamed if they can even bear that, to have done it.

And later, the war is over. People are still hungry. People are still lying. Madame never leaves her bed at all. I look out the window and report. M. Maurice moves out of the attic.

One day Madame tells me I am going to America. She gives me enough money, an old-fashioned but respectable suit she has no use for, and letters she has gotten from respectable friends and her own very proper anti-Nazi letter for the American consulate. M. Maurice gives me a lovely silk scarf, one of his mufflers. Madame gets me a passport that says I am nineteen, and she does not tell me how she got it. I do my part, I sell my two Belperron brooches easily (people are selling everything, and everyone who can buy is buying), and I come to America in leather shoes. I travel in something better than steerage, and I call myself Gabrielle Benamar for a few weeks, but the sound of it, the lie of it, is dirt in my mouth. I talk, if asked, about my beautiful French mother (I don't say she was Jewish because that seems no better than it ever was) and my brave Resistance fighter of a father (I do not emphasize Algerian because I am, as Madame has taught me, a Parisian).

I come to America alone and as Parisian as possible.

Goodnight, Irene

Second Avenue, Manhattan
1947

I have been in New York for six months. I open the bakery every morning. I am happy to be alone in the bakery,
my arms deep in the poolish, the life, the yeasty stew that
makes the baguettes. My boss, Mme. Rouen, my lifeboat
and anchor, walks in for her morning coffee and then walks
out. I know that she knew that I was not a pastry chef, not
even a sous-pâtissier, that I was just a girl with bad English
in an old-fashioned suit, but I showed her the letter from
Mme. Colette, and Mme. Rouen's eyes opened wide and she
ran her fingers over the famous signature.

I am determined, I am polite, and I try to be clean.
Mme. Rouen pays me less than she would pay an American
girl—because she can—and she lets me sleep in the storage
room two flights up. Mme. Rouen washes my smock for me,
with her own smocks. I do my hair in a chignon, every day,
without being told, and Mme. Rouen says that she is pleased
with me, that I carry myself properly, not like a peasant

walking through a field, like the American girls. I do think she is more pleased than not.

I open. It's early, it's still dark. Two girls come into the bakery, wearing corduroy jackets. They look around my age and they look like me, dark, curly hair, thick brows, dark eyes, beige skin, not white, not pink. They are both bigger than I am.

They ask for two brioches and a rye bread.

They look at me for a minute. They look at each other.

I'm Anne Cohen, the tall, sexy one, the big sister, says. She salutes me, like one of the Andrews Sisters, and I salute back.

Alma Cohen, says the other, the one with a sweet face and a dimple near her right eye. She puts her hand out and I shake it.

I hand them their brioches and the rye bread and I tell them my name is Gazala and I see them thinking about the name and the accent.

Oh, French, the tall, sexy one, Anne, says. And then she says, in adequate French, that she hopes I am finding life comfortable in the United States. I say, in my superior French, very fast, that I am grateful to be alive, even if comfortable is still beyond me.

Alma, the kind one, the shorter one, smiles, and Anne's eyes light up. I am French, I am difficult, and I am right around the corner. In a bakery. I am a gift.

The next day, a short, round woman with kind eyes, a black check shawl over her dark dress, both almost down to her brown shoes, comes into the bakery.

My daughters like you, Mrs. Cohen says. I'll take another rye bread, she says. We have a cousin visiting.

I nod. I hand her the loaf.

She puts her hand up to my face, tears in her dark eyes.

No parents, she says.

I nod.

You'll come for dinner.

I nod again.

I do come for dinner, almost every Friday night, and on Saturdays I go shopping with the girls or we walk to the river or we sit in their bedroom and talk about everything. Mr. Cohen comes through the bakery and fixes the lightbulb in the toilet down the hall from the storage room where I sleep.

My first October in America. My first Halloween anywhere. Children walk and run dressed as pirates or skeletons or soldiers or nurses, and there are two little girls dressed as butterflies. They walk in pairs or little packs, holding brown paper bags. The little ones have a parent with them, but some of the bigger boys are on their own (Martians, soldiers, baseball players), and there are a few pairs of older girls with silly hats and lipstick. Adults walk past with no children attached, surely going to adult parties. I myself am going to an adult party, with my new American friends, Anne and Alma. My only friends.

The Cohen girls are dressing as cats for Halloween. They tell me that I must dress like a cat, too. They said they'll come up to my room so their parents won't spy on us.

Slipping past their parents, those good people, is the girls' favorite thing. I can't protest, because then I will be no fun, I would be the wet blanket. But Mr. and Mrs. Cohen are like no people I have ever met, sweetly worried and generous, always sticking quarters into their daughters' ungrateful hands, encouraging me to stay for Friday night dinner when there is already not quite enough food for all of them.

Anne and Alma walk up to my room. Under their jackets they are in black leotards, thick black tights, and old black shoes. They twirl around.

"Hep cats," Anne says.

Alma pulls out a stick of black kohl and we crowd around the little mirror on my wall. Anne does the makeup for the three of us and she gives each of us black liner around the eyes, with big wings at the corners of our eyelids and three thin whiskers on each side of the nose. She has pink lipstick for our mouths and the tips of our noses. Both girls look at me, still in my bakery smock.

Alma says: You're only a cat from the neck up.

My cheeks burn. Stupid American girls. Idiots.

"I will wear this," I say, as if they are the unfashionable ones. I smooth my black smock over my trousers.

Anne looks and shrugs. It's fine, she says. You got a scarf or a belt?

They twist the dark scarf I use for my hair at work around my waist, and no one is unhappy.

You look like Doo-Wop, Alma says. Doo-Wop is their cat.

I lick the back of my hand. I say *Miaou* and they clap their hands.

Alma says: You're so gamine.

Alma elbows Anne back to the mirror. She adds three little black dots to either side of her own nose and does the same for her sister and me. Only Alma has a pair of cat ears to wear, and she's embarrassed to put them on in front of us because she's a nice girl and she doesn't want to be selfish and the cat ears are the best piece we have among us.

Anne says: Oh, Almie, it's fine. Wear the ears, we don't care, do we, Gabi? (This is the name I have chosen for myself in America. It is easy to pronounce and it evokes Frenchness, not Algerianness, and it honors Mme. Sidonie-Gabrielle Colette, who saved my life. It does not last, the cute name.)

Alma parts her hair down the middle and twists each side into a tight and slightly pointy little bun. She does the same for me. We put our arms around one another and twitch our hips like the Andrews Sisters.

"Bei mir bist du schön!" Anne sings, snapping her fingers.

"Of all the boys I've known and I've known some," Alma sings.

Anne tells me: We gotta go. We gotta bring Little David so he can do some trick-or-treating.

A cousin's kid, Alma says. She whispers "Treblinka" and shrugs. Once removed. They are not crazy about David, who is nine and still wets the bed, but he will be sleeping on the plastic-covered couch for the next seven years. Later, David will go to Brooklyn College and eventually become an accountant in New Jersey with a fat, kind wife and no one will feel sorry for him.

Mrs. Cohen says: Have a little bite to eat before you go. Who knows what kind of food there'll be? Mr. Cohen and Alma sit down, and Anne gets the other chair and pushes me into it.

Mrs. Cohen puts down some bowls: tuna, smoked white-fish, herring, and schmaltz. There would be chopped liver, she says, but. I got some rye bread, she notes. (Thank you, Mr. Cohen says to me.)

Everyone begins to eat, and Mrs. Cohen holds up an envelope, pounding the table, softly, with her other hand.

You see this?, she says. I didn't tell you girls, but Dottie, that vantz, got it all.

What?, Alma asks.

Anne pokes her. The Halloween party is waiting.

Mr. Cohen says: Your cousin Dottie inherited a very nice house in Riverdale from your Uncle Morrie.

Step-uncle, Mrs. Cohen says. I could make a remark.

I love that phrase of Mrs. Cohen's. The restraint, the menace.

Well, Alma says, Dottie certainly got lemonade from lemons.

What lemons?, Anne says. Nice house.

Mrs. Cohen calms herself by putting chunks of herring onto my plate, gray, brined fish and sour cream clinging to the onion strands.

Dottie's life, that was the lemons, Mrs. Cohen says. Her mother was the lemons. She was a witch and a meeskite to boot and poor Dottie got her looks. A face like that could stop a clock. Plus, the stepfather. A shanda.

I open my mouth to ask what's a meeskite?, what's a shanda?, but Alma elbows me.

"Sha," Mrs. Cohen says. "Just sha. You three are lucky. Why lie?"

I hope that when I am old and brittle and the only things that still work well are my brain and my mouth, I have Mrs. Cohen's combination of cheerful fatalism and buoyant self-regard.

(In Mrs. Cohen's eyes, why am I lucky? Because I'm not dead. Why are Anne and Alma lucky? Because they have Bessie Cohen for a mother.)

(Bessie Cohen is not wrong.)

I have had, as it turns out, two mothers in my life: Madame and Bessie Cohen. And I am glad they never met.

Little David runs into the kitchen, snatches a piece of rye bread, and yells: Let's go! He wears a derby and carries a cane and has a small kohl mustache. I think he looks like Hitler but I cannot say that—I wish only to please my new family—and it emerges that he is dressed as the famous Charlie Chaplin. He looks at me coolly and takes Anne's hand. He twirls his cane. I hope he gets candy and leaves us alone.

Mrs. Cohen says: He'll run around, and when he gets tired you can let him sleep on the coats.

Anne says: We gotta keep him with us?

Mrs. Cohen purses her lips, and Mr. Cohen, the mildest of men, looks at the girls over his glasses.

We leave, with little Hitler. I could make a remark.

The party is all that Anne and Alma hoped for and better than I feared. There are girls dressed as mermaids, as birds, as bohemians. There is a couple dressed like flamenco dancers. A man has painted his face white and is wearing white gloves. He is miming for a small, delighted group.

Someone hands me a coffee cup with wine in it. A man comes up to me. He is African, with a small, elegantly shaved head, in a brown furry suit with a ring of fur at his neck.

"Lion," I say, and he smiles.

A redheaded woman comes up behind him and rests her hand on his furry shoulder. He winks at me, and leaves with her. Another man comes up, and this man, not elegant, in an ordinary suit, puts out his hand, and, still thinking of the African, I take his large, freckled hand.

His handshake is very strong and strange. His hand trembles. I shake his hand firmly, in what I hope is the American manner. I have never shaken a man's hand before. I have seen Eleanor Roosevelt shaking hands all the time, in the papers, with women and men, with coal miners and even with dirty little children. Madame also supported handshaking when one could not or would not manage *la bise*. Men like receiving kisses, she said, and giving them, of course, but that does not mean you must do either. If you do not wish to kiss a man, she said, you stand like this (and Madame sat up very straight in her bed and pulled her shoulders back). And you look him right in the eye, to show that you have not misunderstood. With a woman, she said, it is much harder to avoid kissing, without revealing the depth of your dislike. Pretend you are shy.

Rick McCann, he says. I've got a tremor. Kept me out of the military.

I am Gazala, I say. Benamar.

Huh, Rick McCann says. You're not from here.

You are correct, I say.

I say the name Rick McCann, and poor Alma, who I know worried that this might be the true end, who thought that she might be weeping at the foot of my deathbed in an hour, laughs.

Rick McCann. God bless him for making us both laugh.

A Guy Is a Guy

Second Avenue, Manhattan
1947

I have seen men in worse shape than Rick McCann, but not in America, so far. Here, babies are fat, children have hair, woman wear leather shoes. Even in America, after the war, there are a few men missing an arm or a leg, but people walk around them respectfully, and the women who look at them look tenderly and the older men make way like comrades. If they have incisions that have not healed properly, that will never heal properly, you can't see the black stitching under their wool pants or their serge jackets.

At the party, I study Rick McCann across the room and say to Anne, pointing my chin at him: Poor guy. I think I sound very American, that spongy sympathy.

Anne shrugs. "Well, something kept him out of the army," she says. "He also says he had to resign from the police. Maybe he was a police officer. He is Irish. They're usually Irish."

Rick comes back to us, and he opens with Alma. Anne

hangs back, arms folded. Alma seems safe to men. A kind-hearted sister, a cousin.

"You girls are pals, I see."

Alma nods. She tries to be polite and kind and she has no interest in Rick McCann. She has less than no interest. He's sallow and sweaty, with reddish hair and a little mustache that he may think makes him look like a movie star. You could argue that Rick McCann will be a little angrier than some other men we've met because he has an illness and didn't serve. The Cohen girls and I do not find angry men enticing. If he hit some other girl, he'll hit you. Alma and Anne step closer to me.

"It's late," Alma says. "We gotta go. Our parents wait up."

Despite every polite roadblock Alma puts in front of Rick, I let him walk us home, and he carries Little David, which we appreciate.

At the door to the Cohens' apartment building, Anne keeps shifting her weight. I put my hand on her arm.

"Rick's going to walk me home too," I say.

"C'mon," Anne says. "It's fifty feet. I could throw you."

"Do not," I say.

It's not the first time that I have sex with a man I don't like. I am determined. I want to undo what I have done, to change the past so that I am a girl who took long walks with a few unlikely men, not a girl who killed three German soldiers.

It's not bad, but it's not what Madame's books said it might be. It's not shivering silk and light from within and waves of desire. I have never made love before, as such, and it's too bad that the first time is the way it is.

Rick's fluttering right hand dances all over my body, down my back, across my shoulders. I didn't expect a dancing hand. His left hand seems to be his actual, sensible, melancholy self. When I hold it, it's like holding a biscuit or a roll. Not bad and, better, not frightening. He pulls off my sweater with his calm left hand. The skin on the back of his right hand blushes and puckers. It cavorts across my body. His fingers brush over my breasts like feathers and I watch them twitch between my legs.

I close my eyes and it is my only moment of liking Rick, of pleasurable surprise, waves rising from my feet through my knees to my center. I hear myself cry out in French.

Rick lies still beside me for a minute and then sits up and says: Bonjour, baby! I curl up around my thin pillow and watch him through my lashes.

Smoke?, he says.

Of course, I say.

He gets up and gets dressed, not hurrying, his right hand quiet, the other zipping and buttoning. I got what I wanted, I think, and I smile at him. We never have to do this again.

It is only when he says "I bet you're glad you got to America, sweetie" that I think of the two excellent bread knives in the bakery and that what I have done before I can do again.

The Cohen girls and Mrs. Cohen and Mr. Cohen, they gave me my American life. Without them I would have stayed the lying, thieving, murderous corpse that I was when I met them.

Habibi, My Love

In the toilet down the dark hall above the bakery, I scrub the Rick McCann off me. It's four o'clock in the morning. I wash my face and my essential parts, swearing the whole time. The sun isn't up yet. The water smells like iron and I smell like flour and sugar and leaf lard. I don't smell like a sausage but I do not, to my own senses, smell good. Madame had square, yellowish bottles of perfume: Ma Griffe, Je Reviens, Tabu. Each had a fat little rubber atomizer, and when she was in a good mood, Madame sprayed Ma Griffe into my hair, just to make the day nicer for both of us.

Mme. Rouen has gone out to buy the cheapest decent fruit she can for fruit tarts, and a few lemons and small bundles of herbs for the savories. I love this time alone in the bakery, with the sun coming up, tinting the sky through the steamy windows. The door is locked and no one will jingle the bell for two more hours. It is the opposite of lonely. It is me, Gazala, and a world that is not painful, not harsh. The poolish smells like sweat and grain, like life, like a field when the sun toasts it.

The doorknob rattles.

I say, over the noise of the mixer: *Closed*. The doorknob rattles again and all my comfort fades. A fist bangs on the door and I know it's not a woman. It could be Rick McCann come back for his Zippo lighter, which lies in my nightstand drawer. It could be Rick McCann come back for more, in a temper over whatever it is that he has suffered and that he now wishes to rain upon me. It could also be the milkman, who has never knocked but could.

Closed, I say again, but I go to the door and pull the black shade to one side. The Open/Closed sign swings against the glass.

It could be my father, painfully thin in a tweed overcoat and a too-large suit, a dark silk tie knotted at the collar of the dirty nylon shirt loose around his neck. He hasn't shaved, but he doesn't have a proper beard, just clumps of black scruff. There is a small dirty bandage near his right, squinting eye.

Habibi, he says, and takes one unsure step toward me. Chérie, he says.

It is not my father.

It is Samir.

Gazala and Samir

Letter from Samir to Gazala: Written May 1945

My little lion,

I write to you from Sétif. Do not come home, if you think of Algeria as home. (I did.) Our country will be a pool of blood for years to come. Ferhat Abbas was my man. I think he was like me, more educated and cutting a better figure, but still, a sensible man looking for a sensible solution to the fact that Algeria was worn out from 110 years of being France's trough, bar, and brothel. He thought it would be a good idea if we had a constitution and if we worked toward becoming our own country. From what I understand, De Gaulle thanked us for our service (I think it is safe to say that more Algerians worked to defeat the Germans than French white boys did) and told us to buckle down and shine the shoes. The French did offer French citizenship to acceptable Algerians (not too Muslim, not too Jewish).

On 8 May 1945, during celebrations to mark the end of the war, our public thank-you-very-much, get-back-where-you-belong, some guys got out of hand. What they

did was the stuff of nightmares (some French dicks were cut
off, and a heartless police captain had his actual heart ex-
tracted and laid on his chest in the middle of the Kasbah).
It was very bad and I would not have been capable of
doing any of the things they did. Four thousand Algerians
took to the streets. Women in white haiks, their faces half-
covered with their lacy adjars. The children. The men,
some of them still in their French Army uniforms, some of
them still wearing their decorations. Young Algerian men
and their fathers and grandfathers. We were celebrating.
We were also protesting, making the point that having
served with valor we were entitled to be citizens with the
full complement of rights. You might think that we would
have noticed how the French reacted (barely) when the
Germans declared that French Jews were vermin, were
subhuman, had no rights at all, regardless of their Croix de
Guerre, their plays, their paintings, their Nobel Prizes. Re-
minder: Frenchmen stole all their belongings and sent the
Jews to die. I don't know what we thought—that the French
could or would, after all, tell the difference between one big
nose and another, one pair of brown eyes and another? A
brown-eyed, curly-haired young man, a Muslim Scout, Saâl
Bouzid, waved an Algerian flag with typical Algerian boy
ferocity, and the French opened fire on the protesters, including Saâl Bouzid, who dropped like a stone, like thousands of others.

I was not among them.

I assumed that things would settle down and that a fat,
French-sounding baker should stay indoors for a few days.

In Sétif and Guelma there were flare-ups, and then the French went mad. I don't think the French troops ever treated German civilians that way (not even in the Great War, in which apparently the French Army did fight). They slaughtered whole families. They stopped pretending that they were looking for terrorists. Colonial military, police, Foreign Legion, the lieutenants and captains from Morocco, from Tunis, from Senegal, they brought in every white man in a uniform and they set whole streets on fire.

They shelled Kherrata. I feel some attachment to Kherrata. It was just a large mechta, minding its own provincial business until it was shelled. Our father had a postcard of the waterfalls of Kherrata on the wall over what was his bed. I loved that postcard (I'd never seen such a thing, water cascading down cliffs). I had imagined Kherrata many times.

Men I had met were dragged out of their homes, or the café, or the pharmacy, and murdered in the street. People said that if you wore a white armband you would not be harmed. This was a lie. (I think this is always a lie. If your enemy asks you to wear something so that they can find you more quickly in a crowd, decline. If you cannot decline, throw a blanket over it.) Men with white armbands were rounded up and taken to the French areas. The police yelled that they had found the murdering scum who had killed decent French people, and worse, and then they let the Europeans do what they wanted to the men left empty-handed in the street, or in the middle of the village, in their pajamas or robes. De Gaulle ordered Muslim farmers and villagers killed by massacre, village by village, and there were so many bodies that the corpses were dumped in ravines or wells.

They built mass graves, a huge one in Kef El-Boumba, but the bodies stank like nothing on earth and they dug them up (those damn Algerians, always more trouble, always more stink) and burned the bodies in Héliopolis. The sky was still black when we surrendered on 22 May 1945. Forty-five thousand Algerians.

I can't come back to France because I will kill every Frenchman I see. I'm doing what I can here. My French lets me go places that some of the men cannot go. It lets me eavesdrop on the French. I've been told that I look Corsican, that I can pass as a Frenchman. I shave every day. I wear a linen sports jacket and a clean white shirt and polished leather shoes, and I listen, everywhere I go.

I would like to comfort you but I have no comfort. I have learned a few things here and I can be of use. Do not come to find me. You would be my weakness, and right now, useful and alone, I have no weaknesses at all.

Let the Lion of Oran come down every street. Let whoever must die, die. Our father was forty. I will not see forty and I am not sorry.

I hope our country will be born before I die.

(Hand-delivered to me by Samir, at last, in 1947. The envelope itself is greasy and tan and folded in half, under a small lion of black clay, in my desk drawer.)

The Luck of Having You
(Mohammed Dib)

Poughkeepsie, New York
2010

Samir and Gazala have rules for their life, for their private life, together, for these last sixty-five years in America. Not at first, not when he found her in the American bakery, and they made a life, with Anne and Alma and the Cohens and then the rest of them. The family. Samir went his almost invisible way, hidden inside the Poughkeepsie department store where he worked his way up, seeing things, buying things, learning the people and the goods. And Gazala went her way, which was contained and mysterious, not entirely invisible. Then they bought the store and they bought a house. And if there were sometimes other women's husbands (never an unmarried man), there were never scenes and she never brought any man into their house.

Gazala and Samir did not call the rules *rules*. They didn't think of them as rules. If you said that they clearly had rules, they would have laughed as if you were truly hilarious, providing an evening's entertainment without knowing it.

Who would have ever told them what to do? They barely remember the woman they loved as their mother (beautiful, pale, elegant, Jewish) and they evoke their late father, that decent man, constantly, but those good people have been dead forever and these two have no children, not by chance, and they have, apparently, no peers. They say so themselves.

Gazala and Samir's rules are: Not below the waist (except to massage a foot cramp or put a heating pad on the small of a back). Yes to the entire back. No to the breasts and the chest. They look very alike, tan skin, brown nipples on a flat chest, and they were both aware, when they were younger, that Samir could drape a scarf across his chubby chest, that Gazala could slip on one of his T-shirts, and they could lie next to each other and see their twin.

Yes to the cheek, no, of course no, to the lips. When people are visiting it's disruptive but pleasant, visits of love and respect. There are noises downstairs often, and later, round, sweet faces come poking around the doorway and there is practically no time at all to do what they want to do, which is lie in Gazala's big bed. (Samir got himself a handsome, dark bed frame, like hers except in twin bed size, to make a show to the family of his solitariness.) They sleep in Gazala's bed whenever they can, and they do, without discussion, break the rules, all the time.

She puts her head on his bony shoulder and he wraps a long arm around her. They both love the sight of his big hand covering so much of her. She pulls, gently, at the tight white curls on his chest. She sniffs him.

"You stink," she says.

He smiles. "I do, I was in the garden."

"I don't mind."

"I smell like onions or shallots, I think. Many shallots."

"I don't mind."

He brushes her silver hair away from his lips. When they were younger, her hair, and her barrettes and bobby pins, were everywhere. In bed at night, she braided her hair and held the braid with a ribbon. The ribbon would fall off in the night and he'd put the ribbons, night after night, in the drawer of the nightstand on his side of the bed. When they make the bed in the morning, they put the two pillows on top of each other and a decorative pillow (a dove on one and a heron on the other, embroidered by Honey, who has, as Gazala said, unexpected delicacy) on either side, to emphasize that the bed is occupied by only one person.

Now it seems to Samir that he has been sitting with her for hours, or days. Three days ago he asked her if she wanted to talk and she shook her head. So chatty, she said softly.

"May I talk about the war?" she says.

"You may," Samir says. "I left you in Paris. I am sorry."

She puts her hand over his mouth.

"You left for a good reason and I became who I needed to become. Not just your little tifla."

"If I stayed, you might have been a tifla a little longer."

"What did Harry say when he was little? Shoulda, woulda, coulda."

She sits up on her pillows, out of the crook of his arm.

She lights a cigarette, a Gauloise that must be thirty years old. The tobacco bursts into flame and illuminates just her profile.

Gazala has taken some painkiller and it has not put her to sleep at all.

I will never go back to France, Gazala says. After the war, to make us look like a country in which everybody was in the Resistance and no one, no priest, no nun, no teacher, no doctor, no mayor, supported Vichy, the government pretended to go after collaborateurs and even the mere collaborationnistes—remember that awful woman in the rue Caplat courtyard?—but really they went after the girls who had sex with German soldiers. Not after Balenciaga, who crossed the street to avoid his Jewish customers, not after Maurice Chevalier, who sang for the Germans. Piece of shit.

She says: I'm glad you were not in Paris for that.

Gazala moves over, settling her bones so that Samir can lie beside her.

It's an early spring, he says. We could do the Seder a little early.

No, she says, late. Make it late this year. And put the tables in the garden.

Samir makes a face that means *It's a lot of work.*

I know, Gazala says, taking off her favorite gold hoop earrings and putting them in Samir's hand. He puts them on the nightstand and she puts her head back on his bare shoulder, her fingers lying on his heart.

Huāxyacac

For Gazala and Samir, going to a resort in Mexico, their af-
fluent, late age had been a beautiful and charming version
of their coming to America. They barely speak the language,
they don't know the customs, and they do not feel particu-
larly welcome. Occasionally, though, just like the last time
they came to a foreign country, someone smiles at them, or
offers help or a new food, and they are quietly grateful. Also,
by 1984, they have money, and that is a delightful difference.

In their fifties, perhaps the last best time in life to be bad
without having to play the fool, Samir had said to Gazala:
Just once, let's go somewhere on a holiday. Let's go as who
we are.

Gazala did not pretend she didn't know what he meant.
To walk with Samir, hand in hand. To lean toward each
other in a restaurant. To brush his spiky gray hair back from
his dark, worried brow. Samir's English had become more
American and highly, unexpectedly idiomatic, and Gazala's

English grammar had improved while her accent had become more French. (Their Poughkeepsie customers love it, she said. Ooh la la.) Samir made the reservations with the travel agent wife of Sam the haberdasher.

They arrive in Mexico City into colorful chaos at the airport, which worries them not at all. They have been in enough colorful chaos to move quickly and with purpose through the edges of the crowd toward their destination: the flight to Oaxaca. They do not give money to the winsome girls selling flowers. They hold their bags close when the boys come by doing cartwheels to gain favor. They packed lightly. They always have.

It is not a bad trip. It's a long way from New York and the flight is a bit bumpy but their standards are not American standards. They do not perish. They do not see anyone die. No one tries to kill them. Gazala and Samir have traveled in America, usually for trade shows or to visit the housebound woman in the Catskills who makes beautiful quilts, or the ceramics cooperative (hardworking hippies, Samir says) in Riverdale. They feel visible and necessary on those trips, they are visiting dignitaries representing the Luckey Department Store (formerly Luckey Dry Goods), making purchases from hopeful vendors. Here they are in an ideal state of being, anonymous and admired.

In Oaxaca, they walk through the town's two plazas. Both plazas teem with people, Mexicans and foreigners, buying,

selling, drinking, looking. People are talking in English, in
German, in French and Italian, and there are constant bursts
of horns honking and people cursing at the drivers. They
brush fingers. They bump into each other frequently, and at
every opportunity Samir takes Gazala's hand to help her
over the cobblestones, around a flower stall. A woman is selling matte black pottery. *Barro negro.* The deep black pots,
flutes, little donkeys, frogs, masks, lanterns, all call to Gazala.
Doña Rosa transformed barro negro, polishing the pottery
with quartz before the final firing. It becomes deeply shiny,
almost iridescent. The new style catches the eye and it sells.
It sells worldwide. When Gazala saw her first piece of the
new, polished black pottery (a gift from a neighbor hoping to
become friends, having heard of the beautiful pots and
bowls that Gazala collects), Gazala wanted to shatter it on
her slate patio. It was compelling, all that deep midnight
shine, and she knew that no one would want the original
barro negro anymore, which is what happened. The new
style is more beautiful and more breakable and Gazala will
not have it in her house. In her house (in their house, she
makes an effort to say), in their living room, where the wall
meets the ceiling, they have two shelves of barro negro, and
on the other side of the enormous room are two matching
high shelves of the green-glazed pottery of Atzompa, tall
pitchers with mermaids, one pitcher very round and large
with a hibiscus splashed across the body and hibiscus leaves
plaited together for the handle, bowls and mugs and a set of
six dinner plates with daisies around the rims, a green clay

candelabra with a horse holding up the four candlesticks. Next to that is a small green skull with a sky-blue fedora and flowers for eyes.

Gazala is a passionate collector of some things (gold bracelets, all of Colette's books). Her adopted sisters and the children think that Gazala's pottery is an expression of her love of collecting and her love of beauty and her love of ceramics and her love of Mexico (where she has been only that one time), and none of that is untrue. But when she looks up at the green plates and the black pots in her living room, she sees only Samir, naked in their carved double bed (more mermaids on the headboard), the sheets pushed back and the hotel windows open to catch the breeze, their blue glasses of sangria beading with condensation.

She sees Samir.

Late afternoon at the Hotel Marqués del Valle. Gazala and Samir sit beneath the arches, admiring the yellow sun, the blue sky, the green leaves on the trees, all as bright and simple as a child's drawing. They exhale, happy and relaxed in this new place, with these new identities, nothing like when they first set foot in America. You can be grateful to the lifeboat, but you are not charmed by it. This place, these tequila cocktails, the restaurant with the red tile floor and redbrick ceiling, this soft, warm air, this is charming. This is what they had wanted, what they had to leave Poughkeepsie for. The waitresses have long black hair braided with colored yarn, and one girl wears her hair bundled on top of her head with marigolds tucked in among her pile of curls. Butterflies and hummingbirds flirt at the edge of the vines around the courtyard.

Samir reads from the guidebook that was in the lobby:
"'The Zapotec were the first Oaxacans, and their name for
the city was Huāxyacac, which time and the Spanish
changed to Oaxaca. The Zapotec were descended from the
Olmec, a people about whom very little is known and who
left the great mysterious stone heads in the jungles of Vera-
cruz and Tabasco. Later arrivals, probably from Teoti-
huacán near Mexico City, were the Mixtec.'"

Gazala smiles, lifts her glass to him, and finishes her
cocktail in a swallow. None of this is like her. As if they were
being watched, she slides her napkin across the little table
until it touches the side of Samir's hand and then she pushes
the cloth closer still, until her fingertips rest on his. She
makes note of every dress, of the heavy white cotton tunics,
of the long pleated white skirts, the multiple necklaces. She
would love to have a store in which the mannequins were
dressed like the women she sees. She would love for the
Luckey Department Store to carry brilliantly colored silk
and wool rebozos, rugs, madly embroidered tablecloths that
acknowledge and then defy loss, grief, and emptiness, pink,
green and orange, green and purple, bright silk ribbons,
bolts of white lace, decorated hair combs, mantillas.

Samir presses the edge of his hand against her fingers,
and then he pulls both her hands into his lap and squeezes
them between his. Gazala gasps and he laughs, delighted
that he has made her cry out a little. He reads again from the
guidebook: "'You may drive out of town to the ruins of
Mitla and visit the village of Santa María del Tule and then
gaze upon the Árbol del Tule, the oldest tree in Mexico, an

enormous ahuehuete, a Mexican cypress, over two thousand years old, forty meters high, forty-two meters round, and 549,020 kilos in weight.' Do you want to go?"

Samir does not want to go. He is a man who loves the odd fact and he is charmed by the idea of the oldest tree, as he is by the small boy who has walked past their table twice, swinging a woven shopping bag and saying something about *contrabandos*, which Samir takes to be smuggled or stolen goods, to which his answer is always: Yes. But he wants only to be with Gazala in a cool room with white plastered walls, dark wooden beams on the sloping white ceiling, and thick muslin curtains to hide them from the world. They will both lie on the bed, after their rest, under the slightly rough clean sheets, feeling the warm air that becomes cooler in the evening, scented with tomatillos and chiles and even a hint of lime. She will let him put his hands under the sheets. She will rest her leg on top of his leg, pressing into his thigh. She will put her hand around the back of his neck, and because she is who she is, she will not pull him to her, she will invite him to come closer, to come on top of her, although they have never done before what they are going to do. It is extraordinary. He feels that there is no need for anything more, no need to leave the room, no need to go home. He is thinking that they can order, if not room service, a few plates. He can make an arrangement with the manager to have food left outside their room twice a day until they leave in five days. Still, they might, after a few hours and a rest, go down to the courtyard for dinner, and Gazala will order three kinds of mole for their colors alone, and he will eat a simple tortilla soup and some plain chicken and the nice dining room girls will understand, immediately, that he has a delicate stomach and they will accommodate him, in this perfect country in which every dish hints at heat and citrus.

Gazala does not want to go see the tree. She might, if they were with the others, actually *suggest* a trip to see the enormous old tree, mostly for Samir and Honey. She might go shopping with Anne, the other serious shopper of the group, and get tablecloths for everyone. She might suggest to Alma that they all take a siesta and regroup in the evening, with a pitcher of margaritas, under the remarkable indigo sky with its twinkling stars in perfect constellations under the faint lavender tail of a meteor that will come that night. (It's called a coma, Samir says.) But she doesn't want those things. She wants to lie with the love of her life and be naked together, naked even though Gazala cannot say much for their nakedness, at this late date, but it is theirs, and when he runs his hands over her small, bony frame, when she rests her hand on the back of his lined neck, she feels that she is a bolt of silk, that he is made for her, that they are a garden in June, that they are the reason people have bodies, they are beauty.

She knew that it would be like this.

Thank You So Much

Poughkeepsie, New York
2011

I cannot sleep. Samir lies very still beside me, his hand cradling his face. That's how I know he's truly sleeping. If he is awake, even a little, his hand is on my hip or smoothing my pillow or he's stroking my instep with his big, knotty toes. Also, he had a brandy after dinner, and I should have, but I didn't because my stomach is even worse than his.

The moon is very full. It lights up my room.

Here is what I see:

Small lumpy pink ceramic bowl for my silver bobby pins (from the daughter of a favorite saleswoman, 1986). Holds six hairpins. Sits next to the chrome bunny-ears ring holder from the girl's mother.

Drawing of a tall thin green man and a short purple woman being eaten by a dragon (or shark or wheat-thresher), in a cardboard-and-macaroni frame (same child).

1950s ceramic vase with a matte yellow finish, cheerful as the ladies' room in a nice-enough Poughkeepsie hotel.

Pale green vines and dark green buds climb up the front, and two sparrows (no idea: nuthatches, finches, starlings) perch upon it. Given to me for my birthday by a good friend who walked out on her husband (he was never my friend) after fifty years of marriage as he was having his morning coffee and reading *The Wall Street Journal*—would this be a completely different story if he had been reading *Das Kapital*? Maybe, if you were telling the story to a man. He said: Is there any toast? And she said: Yes, there's rye bread in the freezer and you can go fuck yourself. Then she took her bag and her car keys and left him. And she came back after he'd been served the divorce papers. Her grown children were upset. I was thrilled. Samir was not thrilled because he likes routine and they, as a couple, were part of our routine, but he has never said a word against her.

Salt and pepper shakers. A chicken with red goggles in an egg-shaped racing car. Given to me by the wife of my dentist, who was my dentist until he retired and my lover very briefly. She brought it as a hostess gift, back when people did that. One of the back wheels of the egg-shaped racing car is chipped because the day after the dinner party (is it a party when you and the dentist gaze at each other with excessive neutrality and your brother and the dentist's wife chat about Paris?) I was about to throw it onto the porch steps to break it but at the last minute I lost my nerve or had a kind thought (it's not so easy to tell the difference, I find) and it landed mostly in the grass, except for the rear wheel.

Three-inch-tall clock designed to look like a beach scene: tiny woman in tiny green one-piece lying faceup, with tiny sunglasses and a straw hat, on a tiny yellow blanket. The base of the clock is a rectangle of wood, painted beige and stippled to look like sand. Given to me one Christmas in the eighties by a long-lost cousin of the Cohen girls who turned out not to be lost and not to be a cousin. He was a lovely overnight guest, full of witty, self-deprecating stories, and he loved everything I cooked. He stole Samir's possibly valuable coin collection, made the bed, and left a charming note thanking us both for the visit. Anne and Alma felt terrible. The coin collection was, as far as I know, no more valuable than the silly wooden clock.

Cheap cubic zirconia watch. Nasty pleather band, a few of the little "diamonds" fallen out. Still keeps time, although I have never worn it. Given to me, at the end of my prime, at the very end of the last moment at which I could be desired by someone who did not already love me, by a man I sat next to on a late-night flight home from San Diego. The plane was almost empty. We didn't exchange names or stories. We each had two scotches, and then he threw his blazer (not a very nice blazer) over himself like a blanket and turned toward me. We slept, his nose pressed into my cheek, his hand on my thigh, my fingertips on his chest. We woke up in New York City and we walked through the empty airport. The shops were just beginning to open. He pulled me into a little jewelry store and bought me the watch. He put it on my wrist and he walked me to baggage claim.

"I love you," he said.

"I love you too," I said. I said it again, in French, it was

such a joy to say something so true and untrue and harm-
lessly wicked. He smiled and walked away.

Samir drove up. He saw the watch and said: "*L'ordure.*"
"Trash." I put my hand over it.

Worn-out pale pink pashmina with stained gold brocade
trim. We carried a line of shawls and wraps in our store (soft
goods, dry goods, case goods, and as French as we could get
away with), and one of the vendors, a very nice man, was
from Bombay. He had two teenage sons, no daughters, no
nieces. The boys were a constant trouble, growing up very
American, and he and I had some lively conversations in the
back room about the foolishness of American parenting.
When his wife died, he brought me two garbage bags filled
with her pashminas. He put them on the counter and I
thanked him. I said I would take care of them and I did. I
put all but the pink-and-gold one back into the garbage bags
and drove them to the St. Teresa's clothing bin. I wore the
pink one every time we expected him, and, every time, his
eyes filled with tears and so mine did too.

When I was a child, whatever I had was given to me, occasionally taken. How else would it be? When I became an
adult, an adult American, I bought what I could, I got what
I could. There was no exchange with a man in my life except
Samir that did not include: Will I? Must I? Can I? And when
I got what I wanted and did not have to give my body over,
I felt clever and lucky. For me and the girls I met after the
war, if you got a few gifts (or groceries, one man in New York
bought me groceries my first month and I still think of him

fondly, despite what it cost me, because for that month I was not hungry and not on the street; because he paid for the food, I could pay for a room, before the bakery) and then he wanted to marry you, whether he was a cabbie or a tailor or a doctor, as long as he was not quick with his fists and not too much of a fool, good for you. Do what must be done. I am an old lady now and I am still struck sometimes by how much some women who live with men loathe them.

Gold pocket watch with chain and fob. 18k. (I tested it myself. A few drops of vinegar and then you know, if you want to know.) It was our father's, Samir said. And yet I doubt that my brother outsmarted Nazis, fled France, survived the massacre of Algerians in Sétif on VE Day, snuck into America, and kept this watch with him at all times. I have no memories of my father wearing this gold watch, and if I can remember my mother's berrad and the gold-wire-and-flower brooch I stole from Suzanne Belperron, how would I not recall my own father's watch? I don't mind. I lie to the nieces all the time about where some bracelet came from, about the provenance of some pretty gold chain, just to make them feel rooted in nice things, in heat and warm water, in appliances and pink bicycles, flourishing in this new world, with the genes of their clever, undaunted ancestors.

The watch has a cracked crystal. The gears are filthy.

Samir gave it to me the day he found me in America. I am, in life and with objects, a repairer, a mender, a believer in the application of tape or glue or a safety pin. I have had that gold watch for nearly seventy years now, moving it from a splintering nightstand to a cheap sandalwood jewelry box when Samir and I bought our first small house, and then to the grand leather box Samir got me when we moved to our big house, which I still own, full of nice things and only a little junk, and I have never fixed that watch. It is my favorite broken thing.

Samir would say: Well, don't forget about me, chérie.

Honey

The Best Bite

Poughkeepsie, New York
2011

Russian dressing drips all over Honey's desk. It is great, biting into her reuben sandwich while the dressing cascades out. Honey is, right this minute, happily rereading *The Price of Salt* in her study, casting an eye over the purple clematis on the patio, sipping a Diet Coke, and enjoying Patricia Highsmith's novel as an old-fashioned lesbian horror-romance. All this, this casually joyful life, spread out around her, Anne downstairs moving orange and red Jowey Hubert dahlias, Harry, the excellent grandson, coming for a visit without his mother, Lily, but with his nonbinary hot ticket of a boyfriend, another bite of sandwich, a little more Diet Coke (a vice planted by grandson Harry, who lives on Diet Cokes plus matcha lattes and bags of organic jelly beans), and some thoughts about a graphic novel she might write: bits and scenes from all the pulpy lesbian romances that were already old hat when she was desperately searching in her early teenage years: *Dormitory Women, I Prefer Girls, Odd Girl Out* (the last handed to her by a sophisticated seventeen-year-old at girls' softball camp who said: It's a hoot!).

Maybe she could do something with those pulps. She could put aside her actual work, dissecting and re-creating leaves and trees and flowers for botanical illustrations, and she could, under the table, feed her unseemly vice of writing graphic novels for a small press run by a wealthy nutcase. Honey's pen name is Belle Burke, and her favorite review said that Belle Burke's two books were "hilariously, astonishingly vulgar and the illustrations more of the same." No need to take Patricia Highsmith apart anymore, she'd done it herself. No one needed to read another word about Highsmith's snails gooping their way out of her bra over the lettuce leaves, to say nothing of the antisemitism and the racism and her enthusiastic, unmistakable contempt for women. Highsmith was like a certain kind of guy, though certainly not like Honey's brother Richard, and certainly not like that poor boy Honey had wrestled into taking her virginity in Racine more than fifty years ago. If you spend time with straight couples, as Honey and Anne do (not as much as they used to, several of the husbands have died), you can spot those guys a mile away. They need women for sex, for social approval, for unacknowledged domestic support (Honey's father, Harold, used to say: I make all the big decisions, like should we bomb Hanoi, Susie handles the rest), but they hate women, and it astonished Honey that women who seemed normal and healthy would and could sit across from a man, day after day, seeing hatred darken his eyes.

Honey sighs. She had loved those lesbian pulps written when she was a baby dyke, when the only proper ending for a queer romance was an abrupt, unfathomable igniting of heterosexual desire or death and/or dismemberment and/or, sometimes, the convent. Those terrible books had given her hope, despite the endings. Women exchanged sizzling glances and they flirted and then they had some kind of consummation. Even if there were tears—and worse—afterward, you could tell that there had been some absolutely smoking-hot sex first. Honey had hoped and prayed and masturbated her way through Racine, kept her mouth shut, publicized her love of the Beatles, the Bible, and softball, and never hesitated to lie right to the faces of clergy and her mother's friends. She had had sex with a nice, tall, kind boy after only three dates (Friday-night movie at the Playhouse Theatre in town; hands held while waiting for tickets; pizza eaten in public; check, check, check, Honey thought), and she had had the out-of-body experience of watching her own sexual activity, like a time-lapse film about plants. His penis enlarged, shooting up like a jack-in-the-pulpit in response to Honey doing nothing but lying beside him in her cotton bra and white panties staring at the ceiling. They had both done their best, conquering her hives, a raspberry wash all over her neck and chest (It's nothing, Honey said, urging him on), and his terrible perspiration (I'm so sorry, he said; Jesus, Mary, and Joseph, I'm so sorry), and they got through it to a companionable end, both of them applying cold washcloths where needed. They went to the prom together, and decades later Honey would occasionally peek onto Facebook to see if he had become a minister or a teacher or gay.

Her friendly face, her lack of conscience, her discipline (no untoward hope and no despair), and another five years brought Honey safely to adulthood, and then eventually to Anne, and the next forty years had been, if not *pure* joy, joy. Honey knew, as most happy people do, that she was lucky. Sometimes she'd shaken her fist at the universe (waiting for Anne to leave Richard, and through much of Lily's, Anne's daughter's, adolescence), but now she never did. She looked up and said: It was *all* fine, and thank you. Sorry I complained. We're square now.

Before Anne, even before Richard and Anne married and had Lily, Honey had had only one romance. Years later, Lily would say to Honey: So what was your body count? And Honey had said: Two. And then she'd said: Three, counting the perspiring boy. And Lily had laughed and apologized for asking. Honey noticed that when Lily asked her actual mother, Anne, about this, Anne changed the subject. And more years later, when Honey's brother Richard was visiting, after wife three but before the Alzheimer's, Lily asked her father and he said: Twenty-seven. Anne, Honey, and Lily were astonished.

Honey's one early romance was Helen Watley, another Wisconsin softball player, who'd left a master's program in Madison for Northampton, turning herself into a Lavender Menace with a sparkly, purple handknit scarf and long dark hair like a raven's wings. Even if you hadn't noticed the long dark hair, Helen had had the word "Raven" embroidered on the back of her favorite jacket and she did, sometimes, mention that people in town called her Raven, which they really did not outside of the consciousness-raising group where women would, out of kindness or in solidarity, call you anything you wanted. Several women tried to call Honey "Huntington," which was her actual first name (Helen had told them), and Honey recoiled but didn't argue. The oldest, butchest woman, a social worker and the group's version of a scout leader, informed those women that they were trying to butch Honey up for their own bullshit purposes, and that was the end of all that.

Everything about that time in Northampton was bliss. Chinese food for dinner and breakfast. Chocolate chip pancakes at midnight. Thrift stores with things you wanted to wear: tweed jackets, serapes, army pants, riding boots. Music and cheap tickets at bars and clubs. Monthly tarot card readings in the Crystal Rose Bookstore. (The tarot card lady answered Honey's question about her relationship by putting down two cards: one for Honey, one for Helen. They were facing away from each other and they were both upside down and surrounded by dead leaves. Honey said: This doesn't seem promising, and the woman nodded and pulled the curtain back for the next worried woman to come in.)

Everything was bliss except the relationship. They were as one with the Chinese food, thrift stores, strong coffee, and houseplants—wandering Jews and Pilea Peperomioides on every worn windowsill and dripping onto their stereo speakers. They had dragged two cracked leather armchairs up the street and up a flight of stairs, and Helen oiled them every couple of weeks. They smelled like lemon and you could slide out of them just by shifting your hips, which was one of the fun things they did, at the beginning.

Honey and Helen themselves were not very happy, but Honey thought that she herself could not be the best judge. Her parents suffered quietly. (Genuinely quietly, she said to Anne later. Not "Jewish quietly.") Helen slept with other women in Northampton remorselessly, as if she were a famous French lesbian and Northampton was the Left Bank in the twenties. When Honey found and cried over a phone number and a pink heart written on a napkin tucked into Helen's jeans, Helen said that she was not interested in the essentially abusive and restrictive heterosexual norms and that she thought they had both moved past that kind of patriarchal bullshit. Probably, in retrospect, Honey, as she was then, might have suffered through and endured the one-two of infidelity and condescension, but then Helen brought it up in their consciousness-raising group, as a follow-up to a woman crying that her partner had threatened to leave her if she didn't get a job. Honey agreed with the partner and said nothing. And then Helen said: I understand. I have also been feeling really stifled lately. And then she made big eyes at Honey, who stood up, grabbed her rainbow-paint-spattered jacket, and thanked her stars that she had been raised by people who kept their misery to themselves, like civilized people.

When she got home, she opened her nightstand drawer, full of Helen's apologetic notes with puns in French. She tore up all the notes and covered their bed with them, like rose petals. Then she went to visit her brother Richard and his wife, Anne, and their little girl, Lily. She stayed for a week.

On the second day of the visit, Honey went upstairs to help Anne make the beds while Lily napped. Anne said: I took the day off, and Honey shrugged. She had a vague idea of what Anne did as a lawyer and she didn't care.

They raised the sheets and the spring breeze caught them. Anne put her hand on Honey's and they looked at their hands as if they had never seen hands before.

Anne said: Come here. The two of them sat on the edge of the bed, like schoolgirls. There was an oval pine mirror in the corner. Honey looked and she looked again and shook her head.

You're like my sister, Honey said.

Nope, Anne said. Not at all.

Playing House

Poughkeepsie, New York
1968

After the first time, Anne and Honey allowed themselves a few days of playing house, once a year. Anne's husband—Honey's brother Richard—liked to fish, and once a year he went with three buddies in September to the farthest reaches of New York State and fished for salmon. The year Lily was six, Richard called home from a diner to say that he was staying an extra day, that he was having the best fishing of his life, and that he hoped that there was room in the freezer for steelhead trout, salmon, and some other large fish that the guys would fillet and put in the cooler, to be shared among the four families. That was the trip that changed everything.

Lily was watching cartoons, sitting on a giant teddy bear, happy with her juice. Honey took note and walked into the kitchen to slide her hand under Anne's T-shirt.

Anne flinched from the cold. Honey jumped back. Anne

took both of Honey's hands and put them under her shirt. Lily yelled, from the living room: Mommy, I am star-ving.

Anne said: Let me make her a snack.

Make her a few, Honey said.

They watched television together, the three of them, before Lily went to sleep. Honey had kept out of the way, staying in her own lane, she thought, except for a good-night kiss on the top of Lily's white-blond head in the hallway. Lily invited Honey to come in for bedtime.

"All of us," Lily said.

Lily said: Daddy likes to fish, and the two women smiled.

Yes, he does, he's very good at fishing, Anne said. It was an easy way to say something nice about Richard.

Do you fish?, Lily asked Honey.

Honey patted Lily's hand. I can, she said.

"Do you like it? Do you catch big fish? Daddy can catch huge fish." Lily spread her arms.

Honey said: Everyone in my family knows how to fish, and then she kissed Lily again and waved herself out the door. She heard Anne coaxing Lily to sleep, singing "You Send Me." Honey's throat tightened. Oh, I'm in for it now, she thought.

"Everyone in your family knows how to fish?" Anne said. They sat on the couch, bare feet touching. Anne brought in two glasses of white wine and a bowl of potato chips. Honey shrugged.

"Fishing?" Anne said. "Really, everyone fishes?"

In the first years of being sisters-in-law, Honey and Anne

had never sat down and talked about anything except dinner and babies and occasionally English mysteries, and they both knew why.

With her long white feet in Anne's lap, and a small bowl of chips in her own lap, Honey said, "Fishing is not what distinguishes us. My parents weren't crazy people. They drank too much, but not by the standards of their community. Those people could put away two martinis, meaning two cups of gin with a lemon twist, serve a pot roast, and leave the kitchen spotless. Including my father, who was good at cleanup and never missed a day at work. But the four of us kids . . . You met my brother Geoff."

Anne laughed. "We do come from different gene pools."

It was a gift that Honey's parents—also, of course, Richard's parents—died so soon after Anne and Richard's wedding, Anne thought. It would not have been a great foursome, the Andersens and the Cohens, and Anne loved her parents.

Honey liked the Cohens, him so sweet, her so worried, and both of them utterly alien to Honey. She smiled at Mrs. Cohen and came up with solutions for her, for life's problems, when she could. She also volunteered to change lightbulbs and adjust the television set. She put pads under the scatter rugs and repotted their indoor plants. At the wedding she talked to Mr. Cohen about baseball, and that is what they continued to do, resolutely, when they saw each other, when Passover and Easter collided or when Christmas and Chanukah entwined. Honey shyly confided to Mr. Cohen that she was a Mets fan, not a Badgers fan, and after that he would brook no complaints about Honey, even after Anne and Richard divorced, even after Honey and Anne moved in together. (He said to Anne: You don't think you're being a little jumping the gun, moving in . . . like this? No, Anne said. I love Honey. Lily does too. You do too, Pops, she said, and Mr. Cohen said: Ya got me there. That's a really nice girl.)

Alma, the kindest of sisters, said: Honey's better than nice.

Tea and Oranges

Poughkeepsie, New York
2015

Honey has loved the musician Leonard Cohen—no relation to her own dear Cohens—for as long as she can remember. The first time she heard Leonard Cohen sing "Suzanne" she simply lost track of the man part of Leonard Cohen, just as she had when she was a girl reading about the Scarlet Pimpernel and Sydney Carton, burying their maleness by inhabiting it. Indigo Girls, Sweet Honey in the Rock, Joni Mitchell, Tracy Chapman, Saffire, Kathryn Dawn Lang—and Leonard Cohen.

Dance me to the end of love.

To a woman who is drawn only to women and has known that since she was five years old, Leonard Cohen is not an exception, he is *the* exception. His poetry, his gravel, his love-me-and-let-me-go slouch, his trilby, she loved it all.

Honey asked Lily to make a playlist for her a week ago, when Honey had a very bad flu, and she listens to it a lot when she is not throwing up or watching *Below Deck* and every other reality show that Harry has suggested. (Harry has sent a hundred tulips to his Honey and also a rare Melissa Etheridge CD). For Anne, who loves Ella Fitzgerald and Count Basie, and also David Bowie and also all of Sondheim, Honey's indie–feminist–lesbian collective rock–plus–Leonard Cohen playlist is relentless. It feels like there is someone in their house burning incense and some other someone (no doubt a mopey ex) making cashew cheese, but it is Honey's wish, and Honey has, as mentioned, had this terrible flu for the last week.

Anne was not put on earth to be a nurse. She carried in mugs of tea and took them away and emptied the wastebasket and bought fifteen boxes of Kleenex and heated up soup. (She called Alma to ask if canned soup was okay and Alma thought it was not but said: Sure. Because she knew Anne, and because she didn't have time to make soup and drive it up from Lakewood.)

Anne is the lawyer you want advocating for you in the ICU when you don't have the strength to insist on more painkiller. She is not the person to make your pillow cool and smooth and she is not the person to meet your frequent emotionally vacant requests with good cheer. Honey knew all this and asked for very little, and Anne knew all this and did her best while trying to hide that she had only one actual thought for the whole ten days: Please, God, let her live. I will do better. Let her live.

Anne calls her daughter and says: I know you must be beat, end of a bakery day. And Lily says: What do you need? And Lily will remember, for the rest of her life, that when her mother asked her for help she gave it immediately and therefore she is a pretty good person, not a pretty bad one as she has always feared. (Lily will sit with her stepmother, after all the years of her just being Honey, when Anne goes out into the world to meet Alma at the funeral parlor, to make a series of small and nauseating decisions about Gazala's funeral. Samir will beg them to handle it all.)

Honey has a fever, and she has, uncharacteristically, yielded to it. It is exhausting but not unbearable, and now here is her Lily, the lanky sprite with the long Andersen legs, the fragile warrior with white-blond hair like Honey's and Richard's (and now shockingly streaked gray), wandering around the bedroom, tidying up and pushing fluids like a proper nurse. Lily wipes Honey's face with a cold cloth, and when the sun begins to set she pulls the armchair closer to the bed and holds Honey's hand very lightly.

Honey smiles, at a distance. She is imagining her own Dead People's Party, as once explained to her by the Cohen girls.

It is, Anne said, just a mental get-together of everyone you've ever known who mattered.

Pets?, Honey asked.

Alma shrugged. In her own Dead People's Party there were no house pets but there were chickens. Hilarious chickens with their tiny green-and-blue mottled eggs.

When Alma and Anne introduced Honey to the idea of the Dead People's Party, Honey loved it. Who is not there? She loved the idea of bringing the past right into the present and that the past brings out the women's girlish selves (sharp, sexy Anne and kind, clever Alma), all giggles and muttered observations, and carries them to their current incarnations, still sharp, still sexy, still kind and clever and also altered by all that they have carried these eighty years and the horizon just a hand's-width away. It takes a while (a minute, an hour) for the Dead Andersens to gather. Hilly, Honey's long-dead sister, comes riding in bareback on a palomino, tossing her hair, bruised around the eyes but laughing. She dismounts with a cowgirl flourish, and Honey's mother hands her a martini. There are martinis at every table. There are tables. With lace tablecloths, like the one Honey's grandmother always put on the pine table for all the Thanksgivings, before she died, before there was so much sadness. Even Honey's brother Geoff, who died in a fire not much different than Hilly's (drugs and stupidity but no one else was hurt), appears as the sturdy, pink-cheeked little boy he'd been: mercurial and playful, making puppets out of anything he could find.

Honey notices that Richard, her last brother, doesn't appear at her party, not even as he used to be. He is gone and now dead, and his Alzheimer's is too painful to revisit and now, as he was ten years ago, dogged, unable to drive or read, mystified by the world in which he found himself at what he thought would be the end, with his fluttery, loyal third wife by his side. Honey cannot for the life of her remember that woman's name, but here's Hilly cantering through the party, lasso aloft, twirling near Honey's father. Harold Andersen, at his best, tossing horseshoes with his kids, sipping on a Budweiser and narrating the game like it's the Rams versus the Browns and each one of his kids is a winning quarterback.

Mecca on Broadway

Oh, here they all are, Honey has called them up: Anne, Alma, Gazala, and Honey herself, all suddenly inside Harry's Shoes in Manhattan, the mecca for women of a certain age, or of a certain condition that often goes with a certain age. Anne had come home from her law office one day screaming her head off about injustice and misogyny, which ended up also being about how much her feet hurt from her stupid spike heels, and Honey, who would have more happily cobbled shoes for Anne, had to offer to go shoe shopping. She called Gazala for guidance, and Gazala said: I will call you shortly, and she called back in twenty minutes. Harry's Shoes, just off Broadway. Anne called Alma, who said that even if she was nothing but the widow of a chicken farmer she could use a decent pair of shoes with arch support. The Gazala who came to the store was not the Gazala whom Honey knew, the sharp and often charming mystery. This was a woman like Golda Meir. Like Anna Mae Hays, the first female brigadier general in the United States Army. In fact, Golda Meir and General Hays also seemed to be shopping in Harry's.

Alma, being Alma, apologizes for taking up so much room with so many boxes, adding, I do limp, a little, and Golda Meir turns to her, tired, hooded eyes blazing, and says: Ya know what, tatskele, we all limp. At that, Gazala takes Honey's hand and they sit down.

Anne did, in real life, buy a pair of black dress shoes, and Honey and Gazala each bought a pair of evening slippers (white doves on black velvet for Gazala, and a gold horse embroidered on navy blue for Honey), and the four of them went back so, so many times.

Honey opens her eyes, sees Lily's face, and falls back asleep, thinking: We all limp.

When Honey opens her eyes, Lily is smoothing Honey's pillow. Honey feels for Lily, who doesn't know how she has become who she is. It seems to Lily that time is running out, and she is right about this, that she has very little time before the Greats all shuffle off this coil and then she will be the grown-up in her life and she wants to do better while she can. Honey wants that for her too.

Lily sometimes says, to her best friends, that she doesn't know how she got to be so lucky, to be where she is (beloved bakery, part of a family, of sorts, not a terrible mother to Harry, a decent daughter to all three of her parents, loved by people she loves), which is much, much better than where she was twenty years ago.

She loved her father and mother and then Honey, her stepmother—although it was years before any of them used

that word, and years more before it was legal—who was and
is probably the best of the bunch and certainly the one most
suited to be a parent. Lily thinks that Honey is that rare dog
person able to translate dog skills into parenting. Nonthreat-
ening eye contact. Holding her own space. Speaking in low,
clear tones. Never backing up or lifting her hands. Honey
rewarded each marginally good behavior every day. (When
Lily was a teenager, Honey did, occasionally, have to walk
out of the room while Lily was speaking, just so she didn't
punch Lily in the face for her clever comebacks. Even then
Lily didn't blame Honey.)

Now Lily says: Honey? Are you awake?

Honey smiles, faintly, and curls onto her side.

"Oh, Honey," Lily says. "You remember Roy? You were
great about Roy. I heard—" (Lily had heard that Roy was
dead, which was good news but maybe not to someone as
old as Honey?) "When I told you and Anne that I was going
to marry Roy, you played dumb, you said: Oh, Roy? Roy
your colleague?—because he wasn't the only man in my life,
which I think you knew. You remember Lamb. Lamb—the
name he used all the time—he was in a band and he was
also a manager at our Stop & Shop. Wasn't he a sweetheart?
Lamb, so gentle with everyone—that shy girl with the hijab,
that old black man, so skinny, with seven gold hoops in his
ears and the bright orange hair. And the old ladies loved
Lamb, you know, circling the rotisserie chickens, always
picking them over, looking for the best or the least dried-out.
Remember, you came by one time. I wasn't expecting you."

Honey nods. It had been an unexpected visit from Lily's

point of view, but not exactly that for her mother and stepmother, who worried about Lily's nontenured, book-stalled,
weed-filled life. They might have gotten the day wrong, but
they didn't. They knew how to act. They were very chill with
Lamb, and Anne invited them both to what Anne called "a
nice dinner," to distinguish it from the awful meals Anne
cooked at home. They'd liked Lamb.

"And you invited us out to that steak house. I have not
been in a steak house in ten years, I think. And Lamb ordered a salad and a piece of halibut and then he apologized
to the waiter, turned to Anne, and said: You've corrupted
me. And then he ordered a big steak and everyone beamed
over the baked potatoes. And Anne said later, when Lamb
was in the men's room: Well, he's good-looking and very
sweet. Maybe not husband material. You remember? And
you made this noise, this great noise, like *How would you know,
Annie?*, and my mother shut up and ate her ribeye. That was
fantastic."

Honey smiles and squeezes Lily's hand to let her know
that she is no longer listening.

Lily sits.

But when Anne made remarks about the unsuitability of
Roy, Honey did not demur. Lily doesn't think her mothers
were wrong. She'd married Roy because he seemed stable.
He had tenure. He had a 401(k). He had never been married
before, which seemed like a plus to her—no stepchildren, no
exes hanging around. Her mothers saw, accurately, a man

who couldn't do the heavy lifting of marriage, and didn't want to, until life caught up with him and the girls he chased were getting younger and running away faster and it was now or never if he didn't want to look like a narcissistic, pitiable failure.

Lily wasn't so young and Roy wasn't so old that their marriage was a scandal. (Everyone had had a girlfriend in college who'd been the too-young flower-faced bride of a man in his fifties, and no one was impressed. Everyone was horrified.) Lily had no excuse. She was twenty-eight, Roy was forty-seven, and he liked to tell his pals that she was an old soul. Also that age was just a number. Neither was true.

Lily wanted a baby, in a hurry. (Anne said that Lily had had baby fever since she was six years old and treated all pets and willing children as if they were her babies.) Lily wanted a stable enough life to make a baby not only possible but sensible. And she thought, reasonably, that Roy was mad for her (not just lonely and wanting to feel young) and that he was a catch—of a kind—and she thought other things for which there was no evidence whatsoever.

Lily would have been better off with Lamb, probably. Anne and Lily ran into him years later, in the Stop & Shop (from which he had moved on; he was in a suit and in a hurry), and he kissed both of them on their cheeks, flirted with Anne, and walked out of the store without any groceries. Well, Anne said to Lily, you must have made an impression, back in the day.

Honey opens her eyes and sees Lily still sitting beside her and wiping her own wet face.

Honey says, "Sweet girl, what's the matter?"

Honey inhales easily and knows that she's better.

Lily is weeping.

"I'm so sorry, Hon," Lily says. "I thought you were dying."

"Well, sure," Honey says. "But not today."

They are the Greats, the pillars of this family, Anne and Alma and Honey and Gazala and Samir. Sitting on the patio, sunning their old faces on the wicker chaise lounges on the big patio of Gazala's house, Honey said: We are Stonehenge, those big rocks. Bronze Age.

They all lifted their teacups to toast one another. Samir walked by and said to Honey: What is a stone hedge? Honey showed him a picture of the Stonehenge pillars on her phone and he said: Oh, yes, this is us. Stone hedges.

Alma and Anne

Bei Mir Bist Du Schön

Poughkeepsie, New York
2014

Only one man had ever called for Alma. Only Isidore Taubman. And as Alma said: No others need apply. Shortish, bullnecked, with a large round head and a large round nose. Steel-rimmed spectacles. Owner of a modest, but not failing, chicken farm in Lakewood, New Jersey.

Izzy was visiting his brother, Ozzy, for the express purpose of buying Ozzy out of their New Jersey chicken farm. Ozzy was delighted to sell his share. He loved the city, hated the country, and hated the goddamn chickens. The two brothers went out for a bite to eat, settle their business, and do some girl-watching.

Alma walked out of the bakery, past the Taubman brothers, and Izzy said to his brother: *Die sheyna maidel iz far mir.* That cutie is for me.

Ozzy, who liked shiksas and went on to marry three of them, helped his brother put his gabardine jacket back on and clapped him on the shoulder. When Alma saw Isidore Taubman get up from his café chair and press his glasses firmly onto the bridge of his round nose, she saw his clear blue eyes and his kind smile and she understood instantly that this man was Her Fate. She knew that her life would not be without troubles, but it would be good.

They courted for six months. Anne cross-examined Izzy, with help from their father.

Anne said to Alma: He's a good man.

Alma smiled. She didn't need Anne to tell her that. She didn't need her father or anyone to tell her that. Mrs. Cohen already knew. She knew Isidore Taubman the way she had known her own husband, Abram Cohen, since the day they'd met. A mensch. Solid goodness. Mrs. Cohen knew that she herself was a pretty good person, but she had a sharp tongue and she worried too much. She imagined un-happy endings. She made remarks. She was not what you'd call a relaxed person, but she had not grown up in a time when being relaxed indicated anything except carelessness.

Izzy and Alma married in the smallest wedding hall in Manhattan. They would have married in the Park, if people did things like that then. Alma watched the 1970s come and go mostly on TV, but sometimes she walked through Ocean County Park and saw the girls in their Mexican wedding dresses or miniskirts, with bangles on both arms, their hoop earrings caught in their long wavy hair, and she loved every moment of it, even when her neighbors were shaking their heads over the bralessness and the guitars. (As Alma said—

and it was repeated all over Lakewood—You don't like to see all that, what God gave them? I got an idea—don't look!)

For Alma's wedding, Mrs. Cohen made Alma a white dress, mostly satin, with a lace insert across the bodice and a short lace train. (What would I do with a long one?, Alma said. Just trip over myself.) Alma insisted on wearing a pair of secondhand but unworn white satin shoes that a neighbor lady was selling half-price. There was sparkling wine and pigs-in-blankets, and as the previous generations of Taubmans had all perished, it was a Cohen-heavy party. Only Ozzy and his first wife, Christina Cross (Really, Anne said, a little louder, for the folks in the back), had a lot to drink. Everyone danced. Izzy did not dance well, but his brother had taught him enough so that he could foxtrot with Alma, who rested her hand not on Izzy's thick gabardine shoulder but on the back of his neck, above his collar. That connection, her fingertips to the shaved back of his neck, was enough.

Mrs. Cohen developed a secret soft spot for Izzy's wicked brother, Ozzy, who could lindy till dawn.

Izzy and Alma had little Renata. Renata was a bubble, a dancing, light-filled bubble, born eyes open. Her name was one of their few frivolous gestures. Her baby clothes were another: pink bonnet, pink hand-smocked onesie, pink ruffled socks, pink-and-white blanket crocheted by Mrs. Cohen. They buried Renata in a tiny pine casket, in her pink baby clothes, wrapped in the baby blanket her grandmother had made for her. The rabbi was an enlightened man. He believed, as lots of rabbis did not, that a baby who died before it was a month old was still a baby and deserved to be mourned. They buried the baby, the other women weeping noisily. Anne and Gazala stood by Alma's side, gripping their sister's hands until all their hands turned white.

A few neighbors, older women who looked on Alma as a real American and therefore better on the one hand and ersatz on the other, the difference between born here and born over there being as meaningful as any other tribal difference, dropped to their knees and pulled at their garments and the grass beneath their knees. Alma wept silently and clung to Izzy's hand on her shoulder. He wept too, pressing his face to hers, and she loved him for that, forever. His grief healed her.

They grieved and went on, as much as people can and more than most, and even though Alma spent three years avoiding baby showers and brises, she always sent a home-made cake, and it was a serious, decorated cake. The neighbors admired her for not showing off her grief by going store-bought.

Izzy and Alma went to Atlantic City once a year on their own, and they went twice with Anne and Richard. The four-somes were not successful. The sisters themselves had a wonderful time losing at craps, winning at blackjack, singing along with the cabaret performers, and stealing every amenity the hotel had not nailed down. (Anne left the midnight buffet with two lobster tails wrapped in napkins and stuffed into the pockets of her dressy black coat.)

Neither man liked to gamble, and they didn't really like each other. Izzy's experience with people in general was not great, and his experience with goyim like Richard had not been promising. One of the pleasures of being a Jewish chicken farmer in Lakewood, New Jersey, was that everyone he had dealings with was, in some way, one of his own kind. Either a chicken farmer, or a Jew, or both. Richard basically felt the same way about people but had his own deep feelings about Jews. The Jewish women he found attractive he admired and feared (just a little). The nice Jewish men seemed to be, to use their own word, shlemiels, and the tough ones seemed like they wouldn't piss on you if you were on fire, and they might have set the fire.

The lack of kindness in the world didn't frighten Alma. She recognized it, and she knew that she had been born kind to bring a little balance. (How many times did her father say *Shver tsu zayn a yid,* It's hard to be a Jew—he said it in response to truly terrible things like a synagogue bombing or a cross-burning and as a joke complaining about nothing: The toast is cold, *shver tsu zayn a yid*.) Alma thought: It's hard to be a Jew, it's hard to be a woman, it's hard to be colored, it's hard to be Mrs. Turner, who lost a leg in Treblinka and lost her big, goyish husband to cancer and still sells tomatoes and squash at her little roadside stand, sitting on a wooden folding chair in front of her barely standing farmhouse.

Alma and Anne went away together, once a year, after Atlantic City, for an overnight. They invited Gazala but she never came and they were not surprised. Atlantic City was, for the Cohen girls, a chance to be foolish and loud, if they felt like it, to eat blintzes at a buffet table the size of a Cadillac, a chance to cha-cha in public with each other (blessing their late mother as they danced) and not worry how it

looked to anyone. They were both pretty sure that Gazala
would not want any of those things. She always thanked
them for the invitation and they always brought her, this
woman who desired only space or objects of great charm,
tchotchkes from Atlantic City, all of which went into one
drawer in Gazala's credenza. When Alma eventually opened
that drawer she found broken-armed starfish, mermaid key
rings, a pair of shot glasses with dice painted on them, and a
glittering ornament of a slot machine.

When Samir calls Alma, he says: I fear this is, as they say, out
of the blue.

Alma says, in an encouraging way: So.

Samir says: Gazala is not well. She's weak. She cannot
climb the stairs any longer.

Alma says: So put the bed downstairs. That is what she'd
done for Izzy in his last months, and it did make life—and
death—easier.

Samir says: I wonder if you could come visit us for a few
days. Gazala always said you are very calming, very steady. I
know you are.

Alma smiles. This is her vanity, her weak spot. At times
in her life, she pictured herself as the lifeboat commander
on the *Titanic* or a deep-sea diver rescuing the idiot who loses
his oxygen tank (she has loved underwater shows since
Jacques Cousteau and his red beanie and the porpoises).
Her Izzy said that she was the best nurse in the world, and
Alma has thought, in the last year, that there is no shame in

running a chicken farm but that if anyone had ever told her in 1948 that she, Alma Cohen Taubman, could be a nurse, she might have been a nurse for real.

Alma Cohen is her father's daughter. She believes in service and integrity. She is indomitably kind but not effusive. (She does not volunteer criticism. She will say, but only if asked: You could do better. Or sometimes she might say: You do look a little fat in the tush, but you're beautiful so who cares, am I right?) She would do anything for her family. Over the years, "family" has come to extend to a pretty wide network, and Alma feels only a little less obligation to her sister's ex-husband, Richard, or to her own great-nephew, Lily's son, Harry (lover of sparkly outfits and show-tunes since birth), than she does to her own dear parents, her dearest husband, Izzy, and her sisters, Anne and Gazala, the people who are the whole world to her, whether living or dead.

Later on, with the success of their department store (a Cohen cousin in Poughkeepsie was a floor manager and the store needed a custodian and a saleswoman, and lo and behold Samir and Gazala Benamar appeared, with the necessary skills and forged references), Samir and Gazala appreciate the Cohens' unstinting generosity (giving when it is not easy to give, Alma's highest praise), their tolerance of things that puzzle them, their acceptance of people to whom they have only the thinnest silk thread of connection. Gazala and Samir reciprocate, when they finally can, with substantial wedding presents, not only for Anne and Alma, of course, but for Cousin David and his fat wife and for Izzy

Taubman's three potato-nosed sisters, with summer jobs for the Cohen girls, of course, and other relatives in the Luckey Department Store, hosting parties on the rolling emerald lawn of the house in Poughkeepsie, with the wicker armchairs and pale green umbrellas stuck into multiple Parisian bistro tables, for all the Cohens and even the Taubmans.

Glitter

1966

One night, a few years after Anne had married Richard Andersen and Alma had married Izzy Taubman, Honey, who had not married anybody, visited her brother, Richard, and her sister-in-law, Anne, and their daughter, her little niece Lily. Anne and Honey sit at the kitchen table while Richard mows the lawn and Lily plays with her Barbies. Honey says, cautiously: Does Richard talk much about our family? (Honey rarely refers to Richard as anything but Richard. Not "your husband," not "Lily's father." Occasionally she says "my brother.")

Anne says: I'd met your folks, of course. I wish they'd been around to get to know Lily. And I only met your brother Geoff that one time, at the wedding.

And be grateful for that, Honey thought.

Honey had been asked to pick Geoff up at the airport in the early morning of Anne and Richard's wedding. Geoff was drunk, sliding down the airport escalator in gold mules and gold eye shadow, his hair permed into tiny, crisp plati-

num curls. Honey hadn't seen him for six years. He had had
three kids by two different women by the time he was twenty-
two, was sued for child support by both of them, and even
served some time in jail for failure to provide. He got out of
jail, gave each girl a hundred bucks, and left Racine with no
forwarding address, no phone number, no nothing. No one
ever heard from the two young women again.

Geoff took to wearing silky T-shirts, gold eye shadow,
and matching gold shoes the very day he moved out of Racine, and you would never have known that the week before,
he'd been rocking a mullet and a Green Bay Packers sweat-
shirt. Honey tried, from a distance, to be sympathetic, which
meant a birthday card every year, when she could find out
his address, and disagreeing, quietly, with her father when
Harold Andersen railed against Geoff's lifestyles, all of them.
Honey wasn't even sure that Geoff was gay. She asked him,
once, on the phone if there was anyone special in his life. He
said: If they got the money, Honey, then they can *be* special,
for a while. Ya know what I mean?

In the car, on the morning of Richard and Anne's wedding, Geoff watched Honey's face closely and said: Oooh, big
sister is put out. Big sister cannot get over herself, babygirl,
and he snapped his fingers near her face. I'm driving, she said.

He wiped off the gold eye shadow in the car and put on
a pair of boat shoes before they got to Anne and Richard's
driveway. He hugged Anne with a Midwestern side hug and
shook his brother's hand with a leer, as if there had already
been and would be depraved sexual hijinks that Richard, in
his prim, sly way, would attempt to hide from Geoff.

One Plate

Poughkeepsie, New York
1961

No one had worried about Anne's getting married. The Cohens worried for their girls, but not about that. They knew that men would want to marry Anne. Despite her being an old maid at twenty-nine with a smart mouth, strong opinions, and a law degree (in 1960, not exactly a come-hither accomplishment), Mr. Cohen thought that, whatever people said, a real man would not find these things to be problems. Mr. Cohen was correct. There had been decent men before Richard Andersen, men who would come calling, offer a trip to the movies or to Salvatore's Apizza or China Star for dinner. The men would come by again a week later looking worried, unfamiliar with wanting. Alma, the family concierge, would open the door halfway and sweet-talk the men back out again, Mr. Cohen standing by solidly. Richard Andersen was a surprise.

In the bathroom, on the day, while Alma put up Anne's hair in a perfect chignon (plain Alma had small, strong hands and a good eye and there was nothing on earth she could not make beautiful), the sisters talked about Richard's odd family, and about the Cohens, and about the point of life.

Alma put a last hairpin into her sister's hair and didn't say what she thought, which was: This guy? Richard Andersen? You had every kind of man around you, the Jews, the goyim, men with heavy beards and heavy accents, men who looked like gangsters but were probably not. You had that guy who acted like Oscar Wilde and was more like Jack Dempsey under the right circumstances. And you pick this guy, Mr. No Harm Done?

Alma put two gardenias into her sister's dark hair, and Anne said: What?

What what?, Alma said.

"I can see what you're thinking," Anne said.

This was true. To the rest of the world, Alma—calm, olive face, smooth brow, mild expression—was impenetrable. Alma disliked many people who thought she really liked them, and her politics were more eat-the-rich than people assumed.

Alma laughed, and Anne said, "You're thinking: Why him? I know."

Alma said only "Moishe Bronfman. I thought: More like that."

Moishe Bronfman was big and hairy, light on his feet, and shrewd. The kind of man who could carry you and your loved ones out of a burning building. Also the kind of man who would be likely to set the building on fire if he needed to and only carry out whomever he damned well chose. Richard Andersen's worst nightmare.

Anne put on Cherry Bon-Bon lipstick, her signature.

"I don't need Moishe. I mean, I *needed* him, but . . . not for a lifetime."

Alma said, very gently, handing Anne a Kleenex to blot, "You see a lifetime with Richard?"

Anne kept her eyes on the mirror. She put Vaseline on her eyebrows, smacked both her cheeks, and put on a little pale pink eye shadow. "I'm not gonna wear mascara," she said. "Can I do without?"

"You can," Alma said. And then said nothing.

Anne sighed. "Almie, you could use a little dolling up," she said. "You want Mama to come in here?"

Alma put on the Cherry Bon-Bon, smeared a little Vaseline on her eyebrows, and smacked both her own cheeks.

Anne said, "I'm a lawyer. You know how many lady lawyers there are? Maybe three percent of all lawyers."

In later years, Anne would pay a lot of attention, maybe too much, to the lives and careers of women lawyers. In the seventies, coming soon, few law firms hired women, fewer still for the lucrative departments, and hardly any women were made partners. Jane M. G. Foster had gone to Cornell, was an A student, and had been editor of the *Law Review* in 1918. Jane M. G. Foster couldn't get a job as an attorney for the next thirty years, and then she stopped trying. She took her smarts and her grit, made a lot of money, donated to Cornell, and got a building named after her. She never got to practice law a day in her life.

Anne would have a series of Norwich terriers, all named Jane Foster.

"What I need," Anne said, "is support. I need a man who will not cry if dinner's late. Or if there's no dinner. A guy who will be proud of me or at least not resentful. If we have a kid—I want a kid, Almie—he could at least throw a diaper on her, if necessary. You know, if I'm arguing in front of the Supreme Court, he can watch the baby for the day. Or pay the babysitter. And no one will get hurt. Richard Andersen. The right man at the right time."

Alma washed her hands and pulled on her white gloves. Alma and Gazala and Honey wore white gloves and pink sheaths and carried small, tight bouquets of pink sweetheart roses and baby's breath.

Honey Andersen was made for this outfit. Alma and Gazala were not. Gazala wore the sheath like it was Dior, not Loehmann's, with giant pink pearls. Alma reminded herself that how she looked was not the point. She said to herself, firmly: Tatskele, you are not the bride. Alma was certainly not this bride, marrying this Richard, for whatever reason. Alma had been Izzy Taubman's bride and was now his wife, and she reminded herself that they had had a very sweet wedding, without goyim staggering about before the bar even opened. She would bring home the centerpiece of pink roses and put it in their bedroom. They would get into bed late tonight and eat a slice of the wedding cake, one plate.

———

Harold and Susan Andersen danced stiffly at the Andersen-Cohen wedding. The groom danced once with his panicking mother; the groom's father danced once with Mrs. Cohen, who made approving, birdlike sounds. (She still liked a man who could dance. No one knew this except her daughters, but she had often, on a Friday afternoon, with a chicken in the oven, cut a rug—a barefoot samba or rhumba or lindy hop—with the girls. Mr. Cohen did not dance.) Harold made a toast. He mentioned his own wedding day (worst snowstorm in thirty years, and believe you me, that did not stop us), his admiration for his own father, who started Andersen Accounting, now the third largest accounting firm in Milwaukee, and the very hard (very hard) work of marriage. He didn't mention the bride and groom, Anne or Richard.

Gazala caught Anne's eye and lifted her glass as if to say: Could be worse.

Where's your sister Hillary?, Alma asked Richard during their one cha-cha. (Richard could dance, which was unexpected and delightful. He kept up with all the dances, even up to the Electric Slide. He mastered that and then retreated to the classics.) He waltzed, more than once, with Gazala. Samir watched from under the brim of his hat.

Richard shrugged. His goal in life, and certainly in marrying Anne, smart and generous and more normal than most of his own family, was to slide imperceptibly away from his own family, to leave his parents without their noticing and without punishment or blame, to drop his brother, Geoff, entirely, without offering financial support or any other kind, and to help his sister Hilly, if he could do it from a safe distance. He didn't worry about Honey. Honey was the best of them. She could manage their parents, their teachers, his stupid friends from high school, and anyone else who failed to see that his sister was the actual goddamn Statue of Liberty, an indomitable beacon of light.

Hilly couldn't come, he said. Last minute.

It was true that Hilly couldn't come.

Hilly Andersen had died of smoke inhalation three days before the wedding. Not because of the wedding. She had been too high and wild for months before the wedding, too much of a mess to clean up and rehab in time for a big event. Harold Andersen wouldn't, and Susan Andersen couldn't. They left Hilly in her apartment, in Terre Haute, with her roommate, and went to Richard's wedding. It was, as Harold said, the only wedding of a child they were likely to get to attend. Hilly's roommate's mother brought the newspaper clipping in an envelope to Harold and Susan, to Hilly's funeral. Susan made a copy and sent it to Richard, who did not attend.

> An explosion during the manufacture of methamphetamine caused Monday night's apartment building fire that left one person dead, four people injured, and displaced more than a dozen tenants. Two of the fire victims were taken to Indianapolis hospitals, according to Terre Haute police. The Terre Haute Fire Department announced the cause of the fire Thursday. The three-story apartment building is at North 12th Street and Lafayette Avenue.

The explosion occurred in the kitchen of one of the apartments in the building when the gas line that was connected to the stove and the furnace ruptured; the gas coming from the ruptured line intensified the fire.

Shelley Keen, assistant police chief for investigations, said that two of the fire victims were taken to local hospitals for burn injuries. Two others sustained injuries from jumping out of windows to escape the flames.

The fire was contained primarily to the apartment where the fire started, said Jack Smithfield, Fire Department public information officer. Some people had to jump out of windows because they had no other way to exit the building, he said.

After Anne and Richard's wedding, after the Cohen aunts carrying their large pleather handbags from table to table, the Cohen uncles smoking their cigars by the one flowering forsythia in the tiny yard, after everyone hearing Susan beg Harold not to have another drink and then, at some exact, predictable moment, a bell rang that only Richard and Honey could hear and Susan walked to the bartender and ordered Jack with just a splash of Coke—after they all left, back to the city or to the hotel (the Cohens had offered to put up the Andersens, who declined, about which all parties felt awkward and glad), Honey and Richard sat down, and Anne and Alma pretended to tidy up and eavesdropped.

The Andersen resemblance was suddenly obvious and meaningful to Anne and Alma. Honey and Richard stretched out their long legs, pushed their horn-rim glasses up on their aquiline noses, and tucked their smooth, shiny hair behind their small, well-shaped ears. All not Cohen.

"Oh, gosh," Richard said. "Hilly."

Honey sucked her teeth, to agree.

"You remember that horse?"

Hilly had had a horse. It seemed to the Cohen girls that what Hilly's brother and sister were talking about was the last time Hilly had been happy, twenty years ago, before the running away, before the multiple rehabs, before the scary boyfriends and, worse, the polite boyfriends who were so scary that they didn't have to act tough at all. Those boys were *Hello, Mr. and Mrs. Andersen, what a lovely evening*, and even Harold and Susan knew that those boys, not even men yet, were evil and unstoppable.

"Ricky," Honey said.

"What?," Richard said, and they both laughed.

"No, Ricky, the meth dealer with no eyebrows."

"They were all terrible. She had terrible judgment in boys, in men. In everything. That apartment. Jesus. Dad made me move her one time. Two garbage bags of clothes and her meth kit."

Honey wiped her eyes.

"For a dollar," Honey said, "what was that horse's name? From Hilly's summer camp?"

Richard lit a cigarette and offered his Parliaments to the women. Alma took one. Honey got another beer.

"Come on, *Ricky*. For a buck."

"Oh, you," Richard said. "You think you're funny. Buck. The horse's name was Buck."

"Ding, ding, ding, we have a winner," Honey said.

Alma brought over a platter of hors d'oeuvres left over from the wedding. She made a little plate for each of them, a platter of Ritz crackers and a pecan-coated cheese ball. She put half the pigs-in-blankets on her own plate and the rest in a pile for Anne, the bride.

Richard was on his second beer and he lifted it toward Honey.

"Hillary Andrea Andersen. She was a hell of a rider."

Hilly's brother and sister talked about Hilly's three summers at horse camp, at the end of each of which was a gymkhana, multiple horse competitions and a cookout, to which all the campers' families were invited.

"What didn't she do," Honey said, "that last summer."

Richard said, "Barrel racing. Blue ribbon. Keyhole. Blue ribbon."

Honey patted her brother's knee. "Down and back. Blue ribbon. Flag race, same. Jesus. Egg and spoon, same."

The four of them sat for a moment picturing Hilly, with the same long legs as her brother and sister and a long blond ponytail flying behind her from under her cowboy hat. (Alma and Anne had seen a few photos.)

Richard lifted his beer again and clinked with Honey. He pulled himself from the past to toast his new wife, who looked, he noted, nothing at all like Honey, Hilly, or himself.

"To Hilly."

They all raised their beers, and it seemed to Alma and Anne that no one ever mentioned that poor girl again.

The Pursuit of Happinesses

Anne keeps a small blue notebook in her bag for all of 1972. She brings it to work and hides it in the glove compartment of her car, a car that fastidious Richard never drives or even enters. She puts it under a pile of Starburst wrappers, just in case. She lays a damp, chewed Starburst on top of the wrappers, for extra protection.

Anne makes notes. She outlines her position (amicable divorce), with a few pertinent examples of deep incompatibility (emphasizing her own irreparable flaws) and a big pitch for their future, separate happinesses. She would have reviewed it with Honey, but even Anne, who is known to go her own way and carve her own path, doesn't think that she should review her divorce strategy with the sister of the man she was leaving for . . . his sister.

She calls Alma. She goes to the New Jersey chicken farm and practices her speech like she's going in front of the Supreme Court.

Izzy comes in and out to wash up, to take two Tylenol for his back, to eat his tuna fish sandwich, and to eavesdrop on the girls. He doesn't love Richard like a brother, or as you could love a brother-in-law or even as much as a good neighbor, but he was never opposed to him. The man held a job, didn't drink, didn't run around, never laid a hand on Anne or the baby. But Izzy has known Anne since she was just a brat, a smart, good-looking brat running rings around all the guys she met. If there was going to be trouble, he was on Anne's side. Also, he has a feeling about Anne and Honey, and no matter how great Honey is, Richard is not likely to be a good sport about the whole thing, whatever it is.

Anne pitches. Alma listens, sitting in a green chintz armchair, leaning forward. She wants Anne to be safe and Lily to be safe and she would be no kind of sister if she didn't want Anne's happiness too. She makes a few suggestions.

Anne pours herself a Tab and sits down, finally, in the other green chintz armchair.

Alma says: I'm just saying, sweetie. Whatever you get Richard to do or agree to, when he finds out it's Honey, his own sister, and when Honey moves in, Mom and Mom, are you kidding me? He's gonna lose his mind.

Anne says: So I won't tell him. Two bedrooms, she's my sister-in-law. She's Lily's aunt. My daughter's aunt.

You won't tell him?

Anne shrugs.

Alma thinks. Richard is not the kind of man to ask hard questions. He wouldn't *want* to know, and it did not seem to Alma that Richard was going to insist on anything more than every other Saturday with Lily, maybe dinner on a Wednesday night when she was a little bigger.

Maybe, Alma says. Maybe.

Anne smiles. If Alma, sensible and intuitive, thinks that maybe Richard will not inquire about Honey's presence, maybe it could work out, at least for a couple of years. They will have to be careful. Honey will have to share a bathroom with Lily. They will have to keep up the separate bedrooms for a stupidly long time. Anne won't be able to go to lesbian parties with Honey, not that she would, not that there are many, but there's always a chance that some pissed-off secretary, or Anne's nemesis, Lorraine Adler, the other really good woman lawyer, who everyone *knew* was a dyke, and who will never make partner because of it, that *someone* will see Anne at the Duchess, to which she and Honey have gone exactly once. But it's the idea of it. She will not have that life of fun and connection with their own kind, people who get the jokes and tell the stories and do Sapphic Charades, and she will not have the protection of Richard on her arm, making her presentable and promotable at her law firm. She will have to live with being private and to make herself believe, and to make Honey believe, that it's not shame, it's just being practical. It occurs to Anne, sitting across from Alma, that it'll be harder to tell Honey about their future than to tell Richard.

In the event, Richard does make it easier and Honey does not.

Richard looked stricken but not shocked (no sex for the last seven years, no objection to his long fishing trips and marathon baseball-watching), and then he spoke kindly, and that kindness, in that moment, kept Anne inviting Richard for family events for forty years, whether alone or with a ladyfriend. Long after the last of the bubbly blondes, it is Anne who visits Richard in the memory care unit, and when Honey and Lily are not with them, she strokes his hand and smooths his white, wild hair and they sing showtunes together. Because he was kind and generous in a moment when no one is required to be that way.

They come to sensible arrangements, and because of Richard's approach (Is there another man?), Anne is not forced to lie through her teeth, although she's fully prepared to do so. Richard does not want full joint custody (which is barely a thing in the seventies), and Anne does not want money (also rare). They do not bad-mouth each other to their few mutual friends or to Lily. Anne compliments his girlfriends, almost flirting, and goes on to do the same with his next two wives, made from the same mold as the girlfriends but a little smarter and a little sweeter.

The conversation with Honey almost kills them. Anne didn't know how to prepare. She did not share her notes with Alma or with anyone else. She was not a cook and not really built for seduction (she'd never had to try), certainly not with Honey, who did most of the seducing. On certain occasions Honey shed her ancient Badgers T-shirt and her chinos, turned on her side, and just looked over her shoulder at Anne, sunlight or lamplight outlining her whole lovely profile. Anne felt this, always at the base of her spine and in her center, and she always responded. Even when they were old ladies and they heard the crack in Honey's neck and heard Anne huffing *Gevalt!* as she wiggled across the big bed, that connection was never over between them.

But not that day, or that week, or for the next six months. Lily's recollection, for the rest of her life, is that Honey came to visit, often. Then her parents separated and Honey was not around much. And then Honey was around more and then she moved into the guest room and then, when Lily was around ten, her mother and Honey fell in love and Honey moved into Anne's room and out of the guest bedroom, which, with its huge drafting table, became Honey's office. Lily has had no interest in interrogating this narrative, as her son, Harry, calls it, though her son, Harry, does and always did.

Anne said: I told Richard. And Honey reached across the kitchen table to hold Anne's hand.

Anne squeezed Honey's hand and held on, picking her way carefully, emphasizing (without quite acknowledging the decision she'd made) the importance of Richard's state of mind, of his forbearance. She talked about the cooperation needed between parents.

Oh, Honey said. You mean you and Rick.

Anne produced a xeroxed custody schedule with bright stickers denoting every other Saturday, which Lily, almost a tween by then, red-faced and contemptuous of both parents, had seen and torn up.

Every other Saturday!, she yelled. What if I don't want to, does anyone care?

Anne says, with tears in her eyes, that she and Honey will have to be careful, and that part of being careful will include being careful around Lily, who has the radar of a bat. If Lily wonders about the relationship, she might tell Richard, probably would, and that might affect his behavior around what will otherwise be—Anne squeezes Honey's hand—an amicable divorce.

Oh, Honey says, you want us to be careful, as you say, until the divorce is finalized.

Anne exhales. Yes, until the divorce is final. Also, probably after.

Honey clasps her hands in her lap. Oh, she says. After.

Anne says: Yes, I mean, you can see, darling. It could be really awkward, a problem. I mean, us. And you're Richard's sister.

Honey says: I understand. Us. Call me if you come to see this differently.

Honey takes out the Easy-Bake Oven she'd gotten for Lily for her upcoming birthday and places a big pink envelope on top of the box. The envelope is covered with hand-painted miniature lilies: yellow, orange, and umber.

Lily likes the envelope so much that she tapes it to her door and keeps it there for a full year, until Honey returns.

Anne and Alma are known to Honey, Gazala, and Samir as "the girls," because they are actually sisters. Sometimes, sometimes, in very private conversation, they are referred to as "the Cohen girls," or even "the Cohenlings." Honey was adored by the Cohen girls from the first moment. All that light, all that length. Honey is respected by Gazala, who is French to the soles of her feet, with none of the Jewish American fear of and desire for blond Christians.

Anne knew herself. She'd married two tall blond Christians, one male, one female—also, embarrassingly, siblings—and when her therapist, Dr. Shlattenberg, observes that Anne likes to be an outsider married to an insider, she doesn't argue. She does say: You do know that I'm a lesbian, a double outsider. Triple, even. I mean: queer, woman, Jew. Also this, and she pulls at her very dark, tightly curly hair. Dr. Shlattenberg says, drily: I'm aware. It is a tribute to Dr. Shlattenberg that during an era when some decent psychiatrists were trying to persuade their troglodyte colleagues that homosexuals were people rather than deviants, Dr. Shlattenberg went about his own kindly and insightful business, treating homosexuals like people and treating heterosexuals the same way.

Blue Eggs

Lakewood, New Jersey
2015

When Shea arrives to babysit the chickens, Alma can go to Poughkeepsie and take care of Gazala. Who knew that Lily's special friend Shea loved chickens and would want to hang out with Alma and introduce his friends to Alma's little chicken farm? He loves chickens. The chickens love him. (And Alma loves him.) Shea, Alma thinks, is their rooster, with none of the nonsense. The hens lay better when he's around. They sit more comfortably; they eat better and all is well. Chickens like order. The rooster brings order; the chickens could have order without a rooster, but, as Alma sees it, just one rooster keeps the whole chicken union from having to negotiate about who's going to be top chicken. The hens hand the job of head chicken to the rooster, who does the crowing and the mounting, the hens support him in his efforts, and everyone puts up with the crowing.

Shea studies the Murray McMurray chicken catalog like it's the Bible. He has promoted the purchase of Crèvecoeurs and Sumatras, and Alma has gone along with him, even on the chickens with curly feathers and the ones with turquoise earlobes. It's not only a joy for Alma to teach someone, a nice young man someone, about chickens and plan to leave her little farm to him and Lily (and Elizabeth), it is also by way of an apology to Lily.

It seems to Alma, tossing corn near Big Silky, waiting for Shea to come up the drive, that she was too hard on Lily and on Bea, Gazala's foundling. She did not care for either of them. Not her cup of tea. No one knew. (Izzy suspected.) There was nothing wrong with them. Only, they were not Renata, her beautiful girl.

Lily was a good girl, a good niece, as far as that goes. Growing up, Lily had had a mouth on her that would have had even Alma's gentle father out of his chair and across the room to give her a zetz to remember. But Alma blames that on Anne's parenting and on Anne's own filthy mouth. And Alma had to come around to Bea, as well. But who is Alma, daughter of Bessie and Abram, to look cross-eyed at a girl like Bea, who saw in their family the goldene medina, the shimmering shore, and swam toward it, hard and fast, with no energy to spare for pretending that she is not determined and desperate to get there.

They are both good girls, Lily and Bea, and Alma forgives them now.

We Wait

Samir has followed Alma's instructions. He does observe that the sister he has called first is Alma, not clever, relentless Anne. It had not occurred to him to call Honey, although she is the stone hedge whom he personally likes the best. Honey is a cool drink of water and Anne is orange juice and Alma, thank God, is a cup of tea. In the end, they will all sit together, all the Greats.

And Alma does make tea. She brings Samir tea, proper English tea and proper Algerian tea, several times a day. Then she leaves him in the living room, in the teal velvet armchair, and she sits by Gazala's bedside, in the parlor. It's not good that a deathbed is so familiar, but familiar is its own kind of comfort. The hospital bed, with its brutal usefulness, spares Alma's back, spares Gazala's brittle bones. The commode is in the corner now; there is no dragging Gazala to the toilet anymore, and Alma is grateful. Those last few trips, in the beginning of the week, after Lily departed (and with something pretty in her bag, Alma assumed with only a little judgment; Gazala enjoyed Lily, especially now that Lily's grown, and why not), Alma let go of her wish to control all the ins and outs of Gazala's house. Alma has put a stop to everything that impinges and everything that prolongs and she works hard to let it be.

She assured the hospice nurse that she could manage at night, and she also lied and said that many years ago she had trained as a hospital aide. It encouraged the nurse to go and to feel good about going. Who would know. Alma had called the Poughkeepsie pharmacy for a hospital bed and all the paraphernalia she could recall from Izzy's pancreatic cancer.

Alma says: Can I do what needs to be done?, and Samir says: Yes, ma chérie. Alma has her eye on a morphine drip for her friend, her very dear, still mysterious, near-sister.

Gazala squeezes Alma's hands. "Make it stop," she says.

Gazala tilts her head toward Samir's armchair. "He cannot."

"I know," Alma says. She is not there to help with life.

Alma massages neroli oil into Gazala's hands.

"My father knew Trotsky," Alma says.

Gazala opens her eyes.

"Yes, it's a true story. Abram Cohen and Leon Trotsky. Blintzes at the Triangle Dairy."

Gazala squeezes Alma's hand. Go on.

"Well, you know my father. Not a fresser, not most of the time, but you put a plate of blintzes in front of him, he wouldn't quit. The Bronx, Wilkins Avenue."

Go on.

"And didn't my father love the Splendid Health and Perfect Eating Academy of New York? And that dairy place? Kampus's Milkhiger Restaurant. Romanian blintzes. Delancey Street. Before you got to us."

Gazala clears her throat and says: Rapoport's. And Alma laughs and squeezes Gazala's hand.

"Oh my God, Rapoport's Dairy. Second Avenue. Heaven. The kreplach. Right next to the chop suey place. You couldn't keep Anne out of there."

Alma said to Samir—a good man, in her opinion, even if he is not as kind or as good as her Izzy—I think she's ready to go. Let's get everyone together and then you decide.

Samir put his long hands over his heart and bent forward in the chair. I will try, he says.

In the end, he sits with Gazala, holding her thin hand, pressing it to his lips, and Alma, leaving the room, says: Call me when you are ready for me to return.

While they are alone, Samir says to Gazala: Let's think about Mexico.

PART TWO

Now

Lily

You Are My Sunshine

Poughkeepsie, New York
2012

Mornings, for old people, vary, but each morning has that moment, between bed and bathroom, the pivotal moment. The crux move, an old rock-climber said; the reveal, the old actor said: when the old person anticipates how things are going that particular morning. The optimist knows that it might well get better by lunchtime, that a few stretches might allow a pretty good day to unfold, and the disciplined pessimist may do the same stretches, the lowering to the yoga mat, the modest dumbbells, rolling back onto the bed for the ankles-knees-hip circles that have served for forty years. But that moment, that question, always lies right beneath waking.

It was not a good morning for Gazala. Samir must be in the garden, dew all over his gardening shoes.

Gazala opens her eyes to a person sitting in her bedroom. Lily, on the green velvet chair in the corner, feet planted, hands clasped. She has the air today of a patient paid companion, Gazala thinks, the pinched English orphan with a rich relative, and although Gazala is very fond of Lily—more than fond—the idea that here is another hand waiting for a gift, another mouth waiting for a delicious morsel to be bought or cooked and delivered, is infuriating and dispiriting.

Gazala turns her face toward the window. Perhaps she'll catch a glimpse of Samir's head, of the filthy tweed cap he wears while gardening.

Lily clears her throat, as if Gazala might not have noticed her.

"Good morning," Lily says. "Samir said you might like a little company, while he's out gardening."

Unlikely that he said that. Or he said it so Lily would go away, because the gardening is for him.

Lily looks over at the armoire.

Aha. The jewelry.

Gazala looks back at Lily. Café au lait, she says, and closes her eyes.

She dreams in French, something pleasant, a field of sunflowers, no one dead.

When she opens her eyes, there is a big bowl of café au lait and a torn-up croissant on her nightstand, with a tiny ramekin of plum jam (she cannot manage seeds anymore, and neither can Samir, so there is no strawberry or raspberry jam and no one complains). Lily holds the bowl to Gazala's lips. Lily smells like the herbs Gazala planted outside Mme. Colette's bedroom window, late in the war, and

Gazala wants nothing more than to give pretty Lily a piece of jewelry right now, something to pick up her very blue eyes. She can give Lily more later.

Lily sends a text to her son, Harry, three red hearts. Harry sends back one big red heart, and the caption is: Save a seat for me. Home soon.

Lily sits with Gazala and passes some time watching her own little play, from twenty years ago.

> Scene 1. The day after Thanksgiving. Kitchen.
> Lily is twenty-eight. Her husband, Roy, is forty-seven.
> Harry is ten months old.
> ROY: Leftovers.
> He looks around for something into which he can put left-overs. He waves his hands to indicate that he's really try-ing. He looks at the half-casserole of sweet potatoes.
> Harry, walking around like a drunken sailor with a diaper problem, waves his arms.
> Lily silently puts a plastic container in front of Roy, partly to help but really because she is already en route to hating his guts, waiting to see what he does next and hate him some more so that she can leave.
> Roy looks puzzled. He moves the sweet potato casserole dish a few inches to the right.
> LILY *(through clenched teeth)*: You can put the leftovers into the container.

ROY *(softly)*: Yes. Darling. Lily. Harry, let's get your doll.
Lily is amazed. Roy has never suggested an activity to
their son, and Lily didn't think Roy even knew about the
doll, which is used for emergencies only. Harry laughs in
delight, hitches up his diaper, and toddles off to the living
room. He flings himself onto the floor with his doll and
turns it on with no help, which is a little disturbing to Lily
but there's no time to dwell on her parenting failures—
ROY: Darling. This *(gestures back and forth between them)* isn't
really working. I don't think I'm making you happy.
LILY *(furiously)*: You're not! I keep telling you—
ROY *(soothingly)*: Yes, yes. I do know. I see it. I'm just failing you. You deserve so much better.
Lily puts her head down on the kitchen table and sobs in
rage. Roy pats her back, gently. He leaves the kitchen. He
leaves the house. Lily hears the car start. He takes the better
car, and Lily simply and absolutely never sees Roy again.
He moves to Dubai, where he becomes the head of a
small English-language prep school. He has no social
media presence, and no one Lily knows, neither former
colleagues nor former students, not even her favorite lady
at the Cuban café near campus for whom Roy lusted in a
professorial way, ever gets so much as a postcard or a
whisper. Harry occasionally says "Da-da" for the next two
years and then never again.

From the chair next to Gazala's bed, Lily texts Harry another, bigger heart, with fireworks.

Lottery Ticket

Poughkeepsie, New York
2012

Gazala and Samir often say that Lily is the pretty one. It's true, and they are glad to say it from time to time, and it hides the other truth: that Bea is more than their favorite, that they consider her to be their own. Anne and Honey would not brag about their own child, and Alma is incapable of making invidious comparisons.

Lily was a very pretty bride and then a very pretty young faculty wife (also a poet, as she kept saying at dinner parties) and then, bam, a divorced, not very solvent single teacher, still very pretty, with little Harry and sitcom babysitters, goofy, adequate college girls and boys getting Harry from swim class to dance class with only that one accident, so terrifying that the fact that it wasn't fatal, that Harry was safe and sound, made Lily forgive the careless, weeping girl on the spot. Lily led a quiet, tiring, busy, not unjoyful life with Harry, precocious and an early reader and the kind of rule-breaker Lily herself had been—sly rather than rude.

Anne and Honey helped her in ways Lily knew she could never measure, could never give enough thanks for or repay. Lily knows now that she's the same age that Honey and Anne had been when they picked up and moved two blocks away from Lily and Harry, and she cannot imagine that she will ever do for anyone, not even Harry—maybe for Harry— what her mother and stepmother did for her.

Her mothers are still their sturdy, splendid selves, and it is Gazala she wants to sit with for the next two days while Gazala recovers from whatever she has. Lily doesn't worry about getting sick, and she won't get sick this time, either.

"Oh, G, I don't think I ever told you." (Lily knows that she has not. Her stories for Gazala are only of triumphs, amusing near-disasters with big-bang finishes and flourishes. Victories.) "I did have one great love. I was almost forty. The universe had given me one more chance and I tried not to fumble it. I knew it was a gift from the universe, because I was wearing a clean top that showed off my cleavage—gotta thank my mom—and my low-rise jeans stayed put, and my ancient cowboy boots, and I think that I was giving off attractive, nonchalant, and misleading vibes at the Associated Writing Program conference. I know it was the universe operating, because the people who were supposed to be (and should have been) representing my college were all felled by various flus and plagues and I was presentable and polite, you know, with my recently published poems—there was one in *The New Yorker*, I think I showed it to you— Anyway, I was asked to go. I went. Thrilled.

"I saw him across the room, at a popular kiosk, a book stand, where they were practically giving away unpopular books and book bags. You know I love a book bag. We saw each other, him dark, me light, him tall and slim, with close-cropped hair and big brown eyes, and we were done for. You know."

Gazala opens her eyes and closes them. She did know. She knew everything that would happen and how this pretty girl—her niece, more or less, this whole family is more or less—had come to be so alone for so long.

"We reached for the same book bag and laughed, and we reached for the same book and laughed again. We each drank half a martini in the hotel bar, and he whispered in my ear about how crowded the bar was. Which it was. The poets and writers showed up at five and didn't leave until midnight.

"So I said: It's stuffy too. And he pressed his damp forehead against mine. We got up and went to his hotel room. I sent a text to Honey and Anne so that Harry wouldn't call me for a good-night kiss in the next few hours and no one would worry about me. I'm sure they did worry, and I did feel bad about Harry, but I hadn't had any real, adult pleasure in so long. Nothing else—decency, politesse, as you would say—none of that entered in.

"Alfred turned his phone off. I mean, not just on *silence*. Off."

Gazala nods. Even before cellphones, one knew the difference between present and *engaged*.

"Oh, Jesus, I still remember every moment of those three days. Everything that troubled me a lot or a little about my middle-aged body, you know how it is—"

Gazala nods her head.

"—delighted him. He traced my stretch marks—my *stretch marks*—like they were silvery, enchanted rivers. He held my breasts like he was a soldier coming home to perfect fruit in his summer garden. Me, I was the fruit. We nibbled, we touched every scar and told little stories about each one. He had a nick in the helix of his ear, he said from when he fell through the front window of a bar because his brother had persuaded him to press his case with some pretty girl and her boyfriend came back to find Alfred doing things. G, I remember everything Alfred said about his older brother. Bigger and handsomer, he said, and I thought: That cannot be. Your brother is trash compared to you. Also, Alfred had a big scar on his elbow from a fishhook.

"Oh, I wish that love for everyone. When we walked through the conference, gliding along, stumbling into each other, we were warm and generous to everyone and we did not give a shit. There was this meeting for all the contributors to the last issue of a famous literary magazine that had included us both— You saw the poem, right? My mother showed you? Maybe not my best work. Maybe not his either, but we did not care. We went to my hotel room and we stayed there. We ate things from the minibar. I'm telling you, I put Ritz Bits on his leg and I ate them up to his hip. I did. We lay there, we took little naps, and then one of us would wake up and fall on the other without permission. We did everything. Do you know what he said to me?

"He said I was so precious.

"And I said, 'Oh, you too. You are perfect. Perfect.'

"I think I kept saying he was perfect. He really was.

"He said he was perfect for me and he asked about Harry. Harry was little then.

"I told him that it was Harry for whom I was buying a red gingham shirt on my way home because he was playing a farmer in the school play in three days, and he also wanted a bandana. I don't think you saw that play."

Gazala does not open her eyes. She had not seen that play and regretted nothing.

"I told him that Harry also wanted red cowboy boots, but that Harry was out of luck."

For his next birthday, Gazala and Samir got Harry the red cowboy boots.

"Really, Alfred thought I was adorable, and he thought I was a good mother too.

"He asked me if I wanted more kids.

"I could, I said. I said I could do that. I could have another kid. I could go camping. Learn to water-ski. There was no stopping me.

"We were, for those three days, everything. Everything: babies at play *and* their doting parents. Air, light. Candle, flame. House on fire and the cascading water too.

"We exchanged numbers.

"Then Alfred said he wanted to see me the next week-end, and I said yes and he said: Really, I'd like to come live with you and Harry, but that sounds insane.

"I said: No, that sounds fine. Not insane.

"And, oh, G, an hour after we parted, I got a voicemail from him. He said: Just reminding you: It was real and it still is. See you Saturday."

Gazala puts up a hand, to stop the story.

"He died in a car accident on I-95, you know the kind of accident that stops traffic both ways because there are so many cars and so many first responders. You know how I found out? A friend texted me the next morning, while I was getting Harry's stupid bandana. She said, *Did you hear about Alfred? So terrible!* And she sent me a link to the local news.

"And then I was pregnant for a few weeks. We came for lunch here and I puked my guts out, Bea was around and she took me upstairs to lie down. And then I miscarried at home, and then I entered the next stage of life, as a sort of workaday secular nun. Good deeds, quiet conversations, regular meals. Like a nun, I learned to bake a very sturdy loaf of bread and no fucking around. I want, I really want, G, to carry my grief like an adult, in a way that doesn't harm anyone but I don't have to pretend. That's all right, isn't it?

"And I'm here every day, better and worse, with the ebb and flow, but you know what I can't do, not for a day, not for one day, is completely leave this tidal pool.

"You know?"

Gazala squeezes Lily's hand. She eats some of the croissant. She drinks some cold café au lait, spilling a little.

Polyamory Saves the Day

Poughkeepsie, New York
2014

It's late fall. The trees are bare and dark, shedding everything, and Samir has put the garden to bed while Gazala watches from the big bay window. Gazala sleeps, when she can, in the ugly beige recliner, which she only allowed to be bought and placed in their house after the last surgery.

Now, she says, this recliner is the rich husband. Awful but necessary.

Lily has come again for the day, and she brings the makroud and the mkhabez that she now sells in a bakery she named Gazala. They are not bad, even Samir says so. Gazala says: My name is chic in America. Now it's an asset. I have lived too long.

Gazala likes to listen to Lily. She liked the martial arts stories of years ago, with pretty Lily throwing people twice her size onto the floor. In the photographs, Lily looks beatific, a murdering angel. Gazala also likes the bakery stories of the last few years. She nestles into the recliner, pillows at every joint. She takes an orange edible.

Gazala says: A good storyteller gives you a world. Shows you what you have seen, what you wish to see, what you have never seen, what you will never see. I am, in my opinion, the best storyteller in the family. But you are very good, Lily. Tell me something I don't know.

Lily laughs. That's not easy, she says.

Gazala says: You flatter me. Tell me things. Tell me how you got to be the lady with a bakery and the friends. Your threesome? Your throuple.

Lily doesn't ask Gazala how a woman in her eighties with a diminishing grasp of English knows what a throuple is. Gazala does, pretty much, know all.

Lily says: Well, I had been in a throuple before, years ago, but now, with Elizabeth and Shea, they started out as just business partners. Breads, pastries, all kinds of loaves. Cronuts. Then we all fell in love. There were a few stages of that and we did keep the bakery going, all through it.

Gazala smiles. You did, she says. Tell me more things.

So I think you must know what it was like. Being broken. I told you about Alfred. It turns out that the only way out of my broken teacup of a life proved to be Garden Party Polyamory, GPP, which is not the same as Kitchen Table Polyamory, KTP, which seemed to me, once it was explained to me, to be the worst of everyday marriage, just more of it.

Gazala smiles. She, too, has not much interest in everyday marriage.

In GPP, Garden Party Polyamory, you have amicable re-

lations with everyone connected to you via your sexual con-
nection to some of the people in the group. For example, if
Bill and Bonnie—these are just regular person names I've
made up—are involved with Mary Lou and I am Mary
Lou's occasional partner, I need to be willing, if asked, to
have an amicable but not enmeshed cup of tea with Bill and
Bonnie, as well as with Mary Lou and, if necessary, with
Bill's other relationship, let's call her Josephine.

Gazala raises an eyebrow.

Yes, even Josephine needs to be included in the general good-to-see-you. That's not for me. Also, I was everyone's Unicorn—I know, I always think I'm special, but in
this instance I really was—the bisexual, poly person open
to joining a couple who is not, emphatically not, a needy
troublemaker. I was also a solo poly, the single person who,
in a phrase I think you'll like, is their own primary person.
So polyamorous people did not want to annoy me at gatherings or dinner parties, or worse, scare me off. I met tons and
it was . . . lively.

Gazala mouths the word "poly."

Yes, but in Kitchen Table Polyamory, as it was explained
to me and I'm explaining to you, everyone's lives are melded,
and it's not enough to go to Josephine's birthday party but
you are expected to show up for Josephine's kid's party, if
invited, or bring Josephine a casserole in the event of a be-
reavement. Not for me. I did not want to be emotionally involved with anyone, let alone someone's metamours, who
are the partners of your partner.

Gazala opens her eyes just to roll them.

Exactly. For a while, after Alfred, I spent more time than I should have at the artsy bar near my house. I could walk home. I was friendly with the bartender and had even covered a few shifts when asked, because you remember that lesbian bar Anne and Honey liked? I worked there after college. And I was old but not too old. I could still wear my hair long. I think I look more like Honey than like either of my parents, don't you? I was not bad at darts, not bad at pool, excellent at chitchat. If I had looked like my mother—wasn't Anne gorgeous back in the day?—someone might have kidnapped me after a second beer and made me a wife.

I baked bread at the bakery and edited that medical journal during the day. I was not looking for a couple. I was, I guess, looking for tall, strong men who could make my backbone slip and then, God willing, put a pillow over my face. Not in the fun way.

Gazala seems sound asleep. Lily goes to the kitchen, pours herself some chardonnay from the fridge, and comes back and lets herself talk.

One night, at the bar, this not-bad-looking man and his pretty wife approached me. He pushed his wife closer to me. He pushed. She blushed. I smiled. Long story short, she suggested I join them for burgers in their booth. They told me their story and how some of the very nice women they had met had boundary issues—which means they did not want to be secondaries, side pieces. Mistresses. And those ladies according to my new friends were just biding their time before they maneuvered their way to wife. I wasn't angling to be a wife. Also, the husband said that they had a One Penis

Policy, which is that the wife can have sex with other women but not with men. I asked if the rule meant that the husband also was not allowed to have sex with a man, or anyone with a penis. They laughed and said that that was correct but also not an issue that seemed likely to arise. We all chuckled because sexual double entendres are to throuple socializing what play-by-play commentary is to straight men.

Lily ambles back to the kitchen, pours herself another glass of wine, and takes some pretzel mix and peanut chikki from the pantry, where there are enough tinned and boxed snacks for a lifetime of international happy hours.

And, you know, we were off. I thought I'd found what I'd been looking for, a nice break from the grief and the bread baking. I used to meet them both at their house. There were snacks—not as good as yours—and then we all fell into their bed. There were the usual thorns among the roses, but since I did not care for either of them, really . . .

Lily finished her thoughts, privately, with tone: I just spread-eagled in the middle of the bed and encouraged them to do their best. I had some sympathy toward the wife, and it didn't matter to me if he was eyeing her anxiously, like the kid who knows he will not be picked for kickball, while she was licking me all over, or if he lost his erection with either one of us. My resolute unwillingness to do a single thing I did not want to do seemed to charm them. I explained that I was a passive person—and wouldn't that have been interesting, if true—that I was willing to contribute some (mostly encouraging) remarks but that my great passion was for being done to. ("Great passion" was misleading, but you cannot say to people, poly or otherwise: I don't love any of this but it's better than death.) Sometimes I'd meet Pretty Wife in a nearby hotel and, several times, at their house, when Husband was away at professional gatherings. Husband, eventually, understandably, picked up a Josephine of his very own, who would not be part of our threesome. Josephine would be available to him and to her own partner, who had several other fish to fry. Husband went from being Not-Picked-For-Team to The Hinge, which is apparently an attractive position, as the person who is the only connection between the other two. Women were often the hinge between two men, or between a ladyfriend and a husband. From what I saw, some of those women thrived—absolute bosses, firm, fair, and unbothered—and some ran themselves ragged trying to find a nice way to say and do what they felt was required to keep the Good Ship Poly afloat: My husband's got a cold, I have to cancel on you . . . again. Or Josephine's upset that I canceled, I need to go bring her some soup and maybe sex but I'll be home in time to tuck in the kids. Guy hinges seemed very comfortable with the position, which usually consists of two people vying for his attention while he does what he wants, until one of the two other people gives up or puts in enormous effort. I did mention, more than once, that the strongest actual hinge is known as a Butt Hinge. I thought that was quite funny. Maybe Gazala will think it's funny, when she wakes up.

Pretty Wife and I had come to an impasse, as people do, throuple or not. Husband was more interested in starting fresh, as a hinge, and he was, understandably, tired of being part of our threesome. Pretty Wife, whose name was Merrill, was, I see now, quite a nice person with deep veins of longing and worry, neither of which was alleviated by having sex with a woman in front of her husband. I didn't feel I could help her, but she did. We went back to her house (I never had anyone in my house except my immediate family) to talk over our breakup with her husband, Allen.

We walked into the kitchen and there he was, Allen, with his new Josephine sitting at the kitchen counter. He insisted we all have a friendly drink together, which none of the women wanted to do, but we did because he was now The Hinge.

Allen said, rallying the troops, that it was time for us to regroup and move forward. Evolve, he said.

I stood up to leave, and as Merrill put her hand out to stop me, Allen gritted his teeth, put his fist to the middle of his chest, and pitched onto the floor, sweating and panting.

Merrill started screaming. I may have screamed too.

The person who did not scream was the new Josephine (whose name was Elizabeth). Elizabeth did everything you are supposed to do. She yelled "Call 911, it's a heart attack!" She chewed an aspirin and put the aspirin mash into Allen's mouth. She rolled him onto his back and began doing CPR, ten compressions a minute, fast and steady until her arms started to shake, and then I took over, which led to a little confusion when the EMTs came, but eventually they left with Merrill and Allen.

Elizabeth looked around the kitchen and began to tidy up.

She looked at me and said: I'm too old for this nonsense.
She said: Clearly, the universe wants me to cut the crap.
Clearly, I said.

"I don't know what I think I was doing," she said. "I
broke the heart of a nice guy, kind of a loser but . . . who
wanted to marry me. I've just been running around like a
dope. Here and there. And now here."

She said she was a baker and I took her out for a beer
and we exchanged recipes.

Nun bread, she said. That's the best.

We stayed in touch, Elizabeth and I, like skittish horses,
texting from time to time until we finally admitted that we
wanted to be friends with no other benefits whatsoever
(which was not true, but it was a good place to start). We
talked about opening a bakery, and a year later she married
Shea, a big sweetheart of a guy. I gave her a yellow crêpe de
chine bathrobe (a peignoir set, really, but you can't even
admit to knowing about such frivolous things) because it was
the most beautiful, ridiculous thing I'd ever seen and it was
in her tiny size. I gave Shea a six-pack of Guinness and a kiss
on the mouth, to seal the deal of our friendship. Six months
after that, the three of us opened a bakery, a proper patis-
serie. I named it Gazala, now that exotic names are cool,
and we used Samir's recipes for makroud, for mkhabez. And
today I'm bringing all the things to you, on a nice platter, as
my mother would say.

I cannot bear that you are all old, frail ladies, which
seemed impossible until two years ago. I can barely stand to
watch your decline and your tender concern for one another.

I hear my mothers worrying about you and Samir. I hear Honey fumbling for her detested and necessary hearing aids while Anne is helpfully yelling where Honey's glasses might be found in order to locate those hearing aids. Richard, lonely to the end, is dead. I think they must have told you. You know that Harry is in Europe most of the time, but he texts me amusing observations and I have started to look at babies with some interest when carried by two dads and I think that Harry does too. My immediate family now are Elizabeth, a great baker and everything a human being should be, and her man, Shea, Irish as a bog and our great champion and now my dear friend, and there is enough love that I think that no one is The Hinge. And we are not poly. We are a dull old family of four. And their brand-new baby, Ryan Andrew. Ryan may be The Mighty Hinge. Elizabeth and Shea are sweet enough to say that Ryan Andrew Shea is named after me, as in Andersen. And you and Samir are my family, at a distance. And my mothers, whose coming absence will be bearable, of course, because it must be, but not really. I do not approve. And I am not resigned, as old Edna St. Vincent Millay, one of Honey's favorites, would say.

Lily says to Gazala: Grief is such a stalwart, sturdy companion, maybe it just wrings the neck of pettiness for us all.

Gazala opens her eyes and lifts her head to look right at Lily. She nods. Oh, leave the pettiness, she says, if you can. Try.

Beautiful

Peekskill, New York
2013

Honey sits in the armchair, by the window, near the bed. She sketches the struggling garden in the courtyard. It is a gift to be sitting in her brother's room again. Richard had done better alone in his apartment than anyone thought he might. He did better than lots of other people in better shape—and he did not get much worse, for a long time, when he moved to the memory care place. One of his ex-wives died, and the one who'd lived helped Honey arrange the move.

"How is it here, these days?" Honey asks her brother.

This is not what she's supposed to say, she knows, but Richard has been staring at her and at Lily, and then at the ceiling, and blinking hard, like a hostage. Maybe it is not just dementia, maybe he's not being treated well. Maybe he is being held hostage.

Lily gives Honey a classic Lily look: fond, faintly critical, not disrespectful.

Richard says, amiably, "Well, it's a fine institution." Long pause. "Of course, I don't think I'm ready for an institution."

His right hand flicks up and down: bada bing.

Richard has never been a big joker. His strengths have been decency and intelligence, and the fact that he didn't know anything about women hasn't made him much different, or worse, than most other straight men, in the view of his sister and his daughter. Anne may disagree, but she didn't share the inside of their marriage with anyone besides Honey, and that was only when they'd first fallen in love and Anne felt she absolutely had to present her case to Honey so that she could leave Richard without being a terrible person—because her wonderful Honey would probably not want to live with a heedless and cruel woman who would dump a decent, intelligent man for no good reason.

Lily takes her father's hand.

He was not a bad father. His taste in women after her mother was always, understandably, the opposite of her mother: They were small, athletic blondes, fading or bouncy, with a martyr's sigh and a complete, frequently announced, reliance on Richard. They were scared of Anne. (Oh, your mother is so smart, one said to Lily, and it was not a compliment. I bet your mother just loves Gloria Steinem, said another.) And, maybe, they were scared of Lily, who was more her mother's daughter than she had thought growing up. But Richard taught Lily to ride a bike, before her parents split up, and he was patient and sensible the whole time, run-

ning slightly while she pedaled and not letting go until she
hollered *Let go!*—and then he did, yelling *You got this, you got
this!* all the way to the end of the block.

That is her favorite memory of him, along with the one
of him letting her do his hair to get her to stop screaming
and running around the house like a wild thing, as her
Grandma Bessie used to say. (Vild ting.) It had been a snowy
day, and both of her parents had needed to work, Anne pre-
paring a brief, chain-smoking and cursing throughout, and
Richard plowing through a stack of papers on *Hamlet*. (Lily
doesn't know how she knows this, but she does. Hamlet, Po-
lonius, Gertrude. All day.) Lily played with her Barbies, built
a couch fortress, and worked on her cartwheel down the
hall. Her mother begged her to give them just a little more
time. Just another half hour, her mother said. And then I am
all yours. You can have your way with me. Lily began to
scream. (She was not a crier.) Richard stood up from his papers and cracked his neck, like a player getting ready to
scrimmage.

"Nope," he said. "Not that. Lily, kiddo, it's dealer's
choice."

Lily stopped screaming.

"Dealer's choice. You choose the activity."

Lily gathered up her Barbie Beauty Salon and put a bath
towel around her father's shoulders. Anne looked up from
her yellow pad and smiled. The snow fell softly. Lily washed
her father's hair (put a wet washcloth on top of his head and
flattened out his thin dark-blond hair). She used all twelve of
her pink foam rollers and asked her mother if she could use

a little of her Elnett. (Elnett was, for the Cohen girls, like pure gold or blue-chip stocks, beyond reliable.) Anne nodded. Richard shrugged. He was already looking forward to his hot shower, his pipe, *The Ed Sullivan Show,* possibly with Anne next to him on the couch but, if not, with a small scotch and watching the show in the den, in his recliner. After the wash and dry and the spray, Lily fussed over Richard's thin curls, poufing them with her fingers and attaching two of her own blue barrettes.

"Daddy," she said. "You are beautiful."

Be Useful

Poughkeepsie, New York
2015

Lily has come to help Alma take care of Gazala, but she's not making a lot of headway. Alma somehow blocks her at every turn, at the side of the bed, at the foot of the bed. The muslin undercurtains are drawn so that the light is not too harsh, and the William Morris curtains are pinned back until the sun sets. Alma does not say "Oh, good, you're here, I'll go downstairs and read." Alma folds her arms.

Lily says: I would like to be useful, and Alma says: Oh. All right. Please get a glass, a plastic cup of very cold water, with a straw. No ice.

When Lily comes back upstairs, Alma has made the room immaculate. She lets Lily hold the cup and tilt the straw.

Gazala closes her eyes and shivers. She hears Alma and she thinks of her adopted sisters, the Cohen girls. Those good, good girls. *Les trois Mousquetaires*. She whispers: Mousquetaires.

Lily pulls out the pashmina, the threadbare pink one with the oil stains on the gold trim, the one she and Bea call the Disgusting Pashmina. Alma nods, and Lily drapes it over Gazala and lays her fingertips very gently on her aunt's shoulder.

Alma sighs. She has been rude to this girl (not a girl) for no reason other than that Lily is young and healthy and sympathetic, with no particular sense of the abyss just inches away from the Greats. Alma feels for Lily, and for Bea, for what's coming, but right now she has no patience with their innocence and their ignorance but will not let herself pierce it, because what for.

Dear Lily, she says. Thank you. Do you think you might leave us for a little? We're old ladies, we need a little rest.

Lily says: I could stay, Alma, while you rest.

Gazala shakes her head, in the smallest movement. She just presses her right cheek to the pillow.

Darling, no, Alma says. I'm sorry. I'm going to bathe her. Maybe Monday? Maybe you could come back Monday. Isn't that your day off?

Lily is flattered that Alma knows her schedule. She will bake like a motherfucker on Sunday, take Monday off, and bring a perfect basket of perfect food. She will call Bea. She can come too.

Bea

Who Even Are We?

Poughkeepsie, New York
1978

Isabel Greene was the first real estate agent Gazala and Samir ever met. She was the perfect real estate agent, from their point of view, and she sold them their store and their house in Poughkeepsie. Silver-blond and in crisp slubbed silk shirtwaists, sensible suits with good shoes and white blouses. Isabel was clear-eyed and attentive to them as buyers, and all silky firmness with the sellers.

Impeccable, Gazala said. Samir agreed.

Isabel sometimes brought her quiet granddaughter with her, and Bea sat in the back of the car, reading, as Isabel drove. Bea came along during the many trips to the Poughkeepsie buildings, accompanying Isabel through empty rooms, quietly scuffing her feet, and then going back by herself to sit in Isabel's BMW while the grown-ups tied up the real estate loose ends. Bea would amuse herself sitting in the big picture window of an empty store, watching the dust motes, leafing through vintage issues of *Reader's Digest,*

which Isabel expected and Gazala and Samir found delightful. (They loved their niece, Lily, of course, and they had met
a few of Lily's friends, whom they did not find delightful.)
They invited Isabel to the house when they were settled in it,
and Gazala said, surprising herself: Bring your granddaughter too. (The first time they met Bea and complimented
her old-fashioned manners, Isabel said: I raised her from a
baby. Sad story, her parents. And she said nothing more, and
Samir admired Isabel's restraint.)

Gazala had collected a vitrine full of Limoges boxes. A
ridiculous habit, she said so herself. But they had charm,
they had the very particular bourgeois charm that Gazala
associated with Mme. Colette, or with Madame's childhood
as Gazala had imagined it, or, closer still, with the childhood
Gazala might have had if she'd been Madame's daughter
instead of the actual, unfortunate Bel-Gazou, Mme. Colette's daughter, who had the personal life that one usually
gets with an extravagantly gifted and publicly admired parent.

Bea, long legs and thick glasses, hair like a jungle plant
and bright new braces, stood in front of that vitrine, sighing,
peering closely at the brown duck on the blue-painted porcelain pond, on the tiny, detailed Monet painting resting on
the tiny easel. Bea's fingers actually twitched, never touching, let alone lifting, that glass.

Samir watched. He admired discipline. He lifted the
glass and took out the porcelain egg carton—with a farm-
yard scene painted on the top, with six tiny eggs inside—and

put it into Bea's shaking hands. She inhaled and exhaled and put it back into his palm. He could see that she was crying.

It is beautiful, she said. Thank you for letting me hold it.

Samir said: You keep it.

Gazala watched from her big teal velvet armchair. "Charming, no?" she said.

Bea nodded.

They all heard the crunch of the gravel as Bea's grandmother brought the BMW around to depart.

Gazala beckoned to Bea, who came closer. She kissed Bea on both cheeks. Samir put his hand on her big curls.

Come again, *Beatrice*, they said, and Bea did. She rode her bike the six miles from her grandmother's house, and when she got her driver's license she drove to their house and Gazala cooked a proper French dinner, and after dinner, Gazala and Samir sat on either side of Bea and Samir brought out a pair of tan Italian driving gloves and Gazala got up and opened the vitrine and took out a tiny bottle-green Jaguar sedan with a minute valise in the trunk. In the boot, Samir said. After she graduated from high school, Bea went to college, and when Isabel died just before Bea graduated from Vassar, Gazala and Samir came to the small funeral and hosted the reception. They held Bea's hand, discreetly. They helped her sell Isabel's house, making a deal her grandmother would have approved of. And when Bea finished law school, she joined a practice in Poughkeepsie.

Bea had found her people. And they had found her.

Kalooz

When they get back from Mexico, Gazala washes their clothes and Samir arranges the pottery and they invite everyone over for chicken and mole sauce. Bea makes her cake, kalb el louz, which she pronounces carefully and incorrectly every time she brings it to Gazala and Samir's beautiful old farmhouse in Poughkeepsie. Kalooz is what everyone else calls the cake.

Every time, Bea sets it on the table and Gazala murmurs the French words for "semolina cake" and Anne and Alma exchange looks in the way that only sisters can, eyes sliding down to the tablecloth (brought home from Gazala and Samir's store in 1972 and cherished through soup stains and cigarette burns and the mismatched lace inserts when nothing more could be done to patch it), to the tomato stain that sits exactly between the two sisters. Then they gaze up an invisible pole until their eyes meet, and even as old ladies they are, like the bad girls they never were, convulsed.

Honey sees and knows and smiles helplessly. She loves Lily and Bea, and she loves these sisters, her sister-in-law almost as much as her wife. She will just plain adore her grandson, when he comes, Lily's little Harry. Honey loves them all the more, and more expansively, because none of anyone's faults can be laid at her genetically disconnected feet. Harry, forever the littlest in the family, a firecracker who is a Rugrat one day, Astronaut Barbie the next, and Indiana Jones Jr. on the third, loves the family dinners, all the lady energy crackling around him.

When Harry is big enough to sit at the table, Bea will be one of his favorite people. She is like Glinda the Good Witch without sparkle (which is fine, Harry will have plenty) and a complete pushover, and she can carry a tune, which almost no one else in this family can. They'll sing "Too Darn Hot" together. They also sing "A Wonderful Guy" and really belt out "I'm as normal as blueberry pie." They sing "Twist and Shout" all through the house, and Bea catches Harry and gives him a smooch, every time they see each other. When he doesn't want to go to sleep for real, he will crawl onto Bea's little bed, off the kitchen.

It became Bea's room when Grandma Isabel died. Bea turned down the guest room on the second floor, politely and because she was not a guest. She picked the small room off the kitchen, which must have been used a hundred years ago for a short Irish girl, which was more recently used for paper bags, boxes to be broken down, twelve-pack cases of seltzer, and reusable grocery bags, and which Bea and Samir then cleared out, and now, to Bea, it's perfect. There is no trace

of her grandmother Isabel's taste, and Gazala and Samir
have filled the refurbished bedroom and the little bathroom
nearby with the nicest bedding and thick bath towels from
the store. When Lily visits, she gets a queen bed on the third
floor and a proper bathroom and shower with a curtain, and
Bea doesn't mind. When Lily visits, she walks around the
living room in her underwear, which not everyone cares for.
Anne and Alma tighten their lips. Honey looks at the ceiling.
(And if Gazala and Samir are around, Lily zips upstairs to
cover up with one of her beautiful, fraying kimonos.) Bea understands completely and envies a little, observing that Lily's
underwear is always clean and pretty, a dark color or flo-
ral print, brand-new and never sheer. The underwear is the
medium and the message, but Bea gets to exchange glances
with Gazala and Samir and she's at peace in her navy blue
cotton pajamas, which exactly match Samir's (Turnbull &
Asser, ordered by Gazala). She is not a visitor.

Lily believed, for quite a while, that Bea had somehow
crept into the tent during their adolescence and that Aunt
Gazala and Uncle Sammy didn't know how to get rid of her.
Bea went to Vassar, a year early, for no other reason, as far as
Lily could tell, except to get even closer to Gazala and Samir.
Bea visited, sometimes, on weekends, when Lily did not.
Sometimes, Lily saw evidence of a visit (a tidy row of let-
tuces in the garden, a new Swiffer in the cleaning closet), but
Bea was not usually mentioned. When Bea graduated from
Vassar, Lily did not attend.

The Greats noted that there was rivalry between the girls.
No one was so rude or obvious as to bet on a winner, but

though Lily had the advantage (looks, confidence, style, and, again, looks), Bea, like a 20-to-1 long shot at the track, had unexpected staying power, which was itself, as Gazala said, not unappealing. Gazala loved Lily because she was a Cohen and part of Anne and the girl herself had all the American virtues. What Samir and Gazala do not say, not to the Cohens, not to Bea, and barely to themselves, is that Bea is the daughter they would not, could not, have, the daughter they can each only imagine, in the most private corner of the garden or when she comes into the kitchen, dark curls on top of her head, blue circles under her dark eyes, standing with her neck bent in the most docile, stubborn way. Gazala and Samir do nothing as vulgar as remark, but they inhale her, they smile at this almost Algerian girl who has found her way to them, as Samir had found his way to the Benamars.

When Lily and Bea were at the end of high school, they were smoking in the garage of the grandest house they'd ever been in. The house belonged to Honey's cousins the Freeholds, who'd abandoned the great timbered Tudors of Duluth and gone for fancy and modern on the Long Island shoreline. Modern-on-the-Marsh, the Greats called it. Even the garage is grand, built to hold four cars, patio furniture, and a second refrigerator on a clean concrete floor. Lily and Bea loved the house's chilly Hollywood sparkle, all pale-blue tinted glass and pale wood and like nothing the Greats lived in. (Boring ranch house for Anne and Honey; Alma in her actual, working New Jersey farmhouse; Gazala and Samir in their ramshackle Poughkeepsie sprawl, where every room had a beautiful quilt or tattered armchair covered by a slightly moth-eaten cashmere throw scented with Ma Griffe, and every drawer held a Polaroid or a vintage erotic post-card and every cabinet had something you'd never tasted before, like pomegranate liqueur or Revolcaditas mango chili candies.) Honey wanted to like the Freehold house, to be a good cousin, but the place was so screamingly, aggres-sively expensive that she couldn't. Honey thought that if her father had been on that trip, he would have found a beer and a chair at the edge of the sprawling bluestone patio and watched the marsh, unless he was needed.

There were swans in the marsh, and beyond that the ocean, and the house itself was certainly roomy, with six guest bedrooms, all the bathrooms en suite, of course, and two more rooms in the barn so that a big family could spend the night, which they did: Bea, Lily, all the Greats, and some Freeholds themselves consisting of the owner, Mrs. Freehold (Honey's cousin), and her two unappealing sons, all never to be seen again. If you asked Honey or Anne or Gazala why they had agreed to visit, having said no several times before, they would not be able to tell you.

Lily and Bea shared the turquoise-and-white jack-and-jill bathroom. Little seashells were imprinted on the bowl of the sink and the floor of the shower. Very nice, everyone said when they first walked in, and only the Jewish aunts made critical remarks. Not actual remarks, just a faint hiss from Alma and a remarkable range of dour facial expressions from Anne.

In the barn, a Freehold cousin says to the girls, snicker-ing: "Uncle Sammy. You think your Uncle Sammy is queer?"

The Freehold boys could not contain themselves. Being gay was not cool in their circle. They wouldn't have beat up a boy (or a girl) for being gay, but it was important to them to show that they were men, or would be, and they were so afraid that they'd fail, that at seventeen they had already failed, that they yelled louder and punched each other until Lily stopped them.

"Really?" Lily said. "My mothers are lesbians. Your own cousin Honey, right? I might be one too. Scared?" She wiggled her fingers at them.

The boys were trying to find the right posture, because Lily was shockingly pretty and tall and cold-eyed and Bea seemed oddly undaunted for a nerd.

"Calm down," the shorter boy said. "We were just kidding around."

Samir suddenly loomed up behind him, if a thin old man in a worn white Brooks Brothers shirt and khakis with grass stains could loom.

Samir took the taller boy, Michael, by the neck, and the girls could see that the grip was not gentle. It was not a reprimand. It was a warning.

"Michael," he said. "It is Michael, yes?"

All of them understood that Samir had heard it all and didn't care which boy it was, that the boys were all the same to him, gnats who had come upon him, through a miscalculation, an error on his own part. He should never have agreed to make this trip to Long Island, to see this absurd pile of glass overlooking a swamp, to extend himself and Gazala to the rich and idiotic cousin of dear Honey, for whom he cares deeply. He tightens his grip on the chubby white neck.

"Ah, jeez, sir. Umm. I'm sorry. We were just kidding."

Michael's head hung down and they saw the red dents on his neck, under Samir's fingers.

"Just kidding," the other boy said. "We didn't mean anything."

Samir opened his hand, flinging the boy away.

"*Défendez-vous,*" he said. "Be a man. If you believe something, stand by it. *Pitoyables.*"

Samir walked away, leaning a little on his cane, which Bea knew—and had told no one—has a sword within it. You press the small, jeweled metal button, push it to one side on its thin metal track, and the sword emerges, with a few nicks and no tarnish. Bea longed for the sword and she discovered, right then in the barn, that she longed to see Samir use it on that boy.

That night, in the tone-on-tone perfection of the fancy house, under the turquoise duvets and starfish pillows, Bea said to Lily: "I wish Samir had beat the shit out of those boys. I should have said something."

"That's not you," Lily said. "Next time, I'll take care of it."

There was never a next time with those boys, but both girls sometimes dreamt of one more crippling encounter.

Lily and Bea sat in the backseat all the way home to Poughkeepsie, reading, barefoot, sharing a bag of Milka's Choco Wafers.

Better and Worse

Poughkeepsie, New York
1996

Bea's wedding was a mistake and she knew it. She had imagined a perfect summer day, a Mexican wedding dress, parents whom she barely remembered magically returned to this world, her grandmother still alive and kinder, and Bea herself with someone she loves past all expression. Robert is not that man.

Bea has been sitting for an hour on a hard kitchen chair inside Gazala's house getting her hair pushed into a twist by Alma, letting Lily do her eyebrows, wishing she had picked better music and a different dress, feeling like a woman who's gotten off at the wrong bus stop.

Her cousin Jess, the only cousin that she's aware of, has come. He came to her high school graduation and to her college graduation. He represents her parents and her grandmother, and he seems happy to do it when needed. With his slightly old-fashioned handsomeness (neat beard, strong brow, excellent posture), Jess is the standout male, ev-

eryone's first choice for opening the champagne and escort-
ing the wobbly. He has been the outstanding male for so
long that their grandmother never even referred to his first
nineteen years as a girl, and Bea has only ever known him as
him, as Cousin Jess. He is the husband of Naomi, as essentially female and feminine as Jess is male and masculine, and
he is the father of little twins Luke and Lisa. Bea never thinks
of Jess being trans at all, except when someone who should
know better seems to recoil at the idea of trans, or when
someone, instead of recoiling, is loudly and persistently *fas-
cinated*. When people complain about being stuck in some
stage or role in life, complaining about how hard it is, how
much psychological work it is to go from choir to choirmas-
ter, from married to single, from lawyer to organic farmer,
Bea thinks: You should meet my cousin Jess. Jeez. Cousin
Jess offers to walk her down the aisle, but Bea declines.
Gazala offers up Samir and Bea declines, to be polite to
Cousin Jess, and that is one of those errors in judgment that
we all make and remember.

Bea's grandmother Isabel is long gone, and Bea is still
comforted by Isabel's remarks bouncing around Bea's inte-
rior. In this case, Isabel says: That poor woman (the minister), mutton dressed as lamb. Bea says this to Anne, who
snickers. Alma tries not to smile. Gazala has been on the
porch, smoking, and mutters, *Habillez-vous à votre âge. Ma foi.*

There is nothing white at this wedding except the smallest cousin's party dress, embroidered with tiny daisies and
finished off with dazzlingly white high-tops. It's a small
crowd, in Bea's own backyard. Robert's mother sits in the

front row, and she seems matter-of-factly and permanently grief-stricken—like Lily, Bea thinks as Lily sits in the second row, shoulder to shoulder with Harry, who is in a sailor suit. Bea can't imagine why or even how Lily could be grief-stricken, could be anything except sublimely self-confident, until she sees Lily's pale, tight face and is moved, without liking her any better.

It will be a little while longer before those two can actually see each other.

Alma offers to act as nanny for the whole wedding.

Alma says, "Children are a joy. Just put me at a little table with them, if you want." Which is what they do, and there will be one photo of a boy on Alma's shoulder, limp as a dishtowel, while she holds a girl's bare feet in her other hand so that the girl can do a handstand. Alma looks, as she usually does, peaceful and curious.

Bea's grandmother had not been a baby person, but Bea was one, although it took a while for her to live with that, considering. The marriage to Robert turned out to have been mostly for babies, and the babies didn't come.

Bea's about-to-be-husband, Robert, was, as Bea said, as Anne and Alma and Honey agreed, a perfectly nice man. Gazala was not asked her opinion and she did not volunteer it and there was no one who did not know what she thought. Robert had invited his entire family, and they drove a caravan of RVs to the small house Bea had just bought, filling the circular driveway until the caterers begged them to move to the street, which they did, crushing the old blue hydrangeas. Robert's mother had a migraine the morning of the wedding and stayed in her RV until five minutes before the ceremony. She came out, limply, and wore sunglasses until after they cut the cake, and then she went back into the RV. Robert's father sat on the patio, expressing irritation about the long drive and the number of people he had to be nice to. That irritation led him to start drinking scotch at nine A.M., which led to him slipping on the back stairs, which led to a burgundy leather wedding album filled with photos of Robert's father looking as if he'd been in medieval battle (torn ear, bloodied cheek, bandaged hand). Otherwise the wedding was picture-perfect, as was Bea, although Bea would not believe that until she was fifty and looking through the album after cleaning out the attic of the small house. At fifty, she could finally say: Are you kidding me?, look at that ass. Bea was perfect then, face like a peony, silky black curls, and if you'd smacked that ass, that ass would have smacked you back.

Robert's father was a brute. A charming brute. Bea could see it from the moment he stepped out of the RV. Bea wouldn't marry a brute, but she knew that she had been willing to date brutes and forgive them too quickly, minimizing their offenses and then weaseling out of the relationship by feigning whatever she had to feign. Bea hoped it was because she had never known her father or her grandfather and just kept mistaking height and broad shoulders for strength and maturity. She hoped it was that.

As the sun was setting, Bea saw Robert and his father drinking side by side and she had as much of an epiphany as one is likely to get in this confusing world. She headed straight for Robert to suggest, to recommend as strongly and politely as possible, that they catch the Unitarian minister on her way out and get the wedding annulled or canceled, whatever Unitarians did. But Robert's father grabbed Bea around the waist and then rested his big ribeye hands on Bea's nearly bare shoulders, just leaving them there until Bea was blinking in shock, and then Alma had had enough and dropped a bristling, oily coconut shrimp onto his jacket. Robert blanched and Robert's father looked at the trail of oil drops as if someone should do something about it, and fast.

Gazala pressed a napkin into his hand, smiling. Nothing would take oil out of silk.

"Those shrimp," Gazala said. *"Dangereuses."*

Alma said to Bea, "Go get your tall glass of milk. Poor Robert."

Bea lost her nerve. She felt sorry for Poor Robert, from the slippery bottoms of her silk sandals to the top of the baby's breath crowning her hair.

Robert and Bea sat down with Alma, Izzy, Honey, and Anne (Samir and Gazala sat in the last of the sun, straw fedora on him, black straw cartwheel hat on her), and as soon as they sat down Bea knew that she should have just kept ambling through the yard. All of the Greats were three glasses in, and the wine, and the pretty June weather and the chance to sit down and take off their shoes (even Honey's Birkenstocks), had gotten to them.

Anne whispered something to Alma, and they screamed with laughter. That is not a figure of speech. People fifty yards away turned around, to see if there were seagulls. Alma then whispered to Honey, who hooted, and before Bea could shut him up, Robert, in the stilted, slightly hostile tone that people have when faced with other people's hysterical laughter, asked them what was so funny.

"Oh my God, my God. It's just—" said Anne.

Alma said, "You know, it's just the Dead People's Party. I said to her that this was even better than the Dead People's Party, because we're alive but you know . . . on the cusp."

"The Arbitmans," Anne screamed.

Alma wiped away tears of laughter. "Weren't they perfect? Like salt and pepper shakers. Tiny, neat, their feet barely touched the floor."

Izzy Taubman smiled. He loved these girls.

"That immaculate floor," Honey said, smiling over people she had never met. "They lived across the hall from the Cohens. The cutest, tiniest, nicest people ever."

"Her stuffed cabbage," Anne said.

"It was perfection," Gazala said, from across the lawn. Samir raised his glass.

Bea knew about the Arbitmans. If you were in this extended family, you knew about the Cohen sisters and their Dead People's Party, which included everyone that any of the Greats had ever known and cherished, and even not cherished but just remembered fondly. Or strongly disliked. There was a table for them too, with noticeably bad service and worse food. Anne once said: We know it's not funny to anyone else. We don't care. You've got your nonsense, we've got ours.

"Butchie," Alma said. "Their dog."

"He scared me," Anne said. "Huge dog. An Italian mastiff. A Cane Corso."

"Oh, for God's sake," Alma said. "In what universe did the Arbitmans have a giant Italian dog? He would have eaten them. Butchie was a mutt. Maybe, *maybe* a boxer."

They turned to Robert, telling him about things he didn't care to know, talking over each other.

It's not a bad thing, Alma once told Bea, the talking over, the interrupting. It's Cooperative Overlapping. Sociologists say so. Enthusiastic listening. It's a good thing. Jews do it, that's true. Black people do it too. And Italians. Italians, Anne said, maybe to a fault.

Fool Me Once

Poughkeepsie, New York
2008

When Bea embarked on her affair with Eli, after the brief marriage to Poor Robert, as the entire family referred to him forever, she gave herself a talking-to. She told herself that this affair, a fling with a lawyer in a different firm but the same building, was a chance to have fun, to have sex and do no real harm. It turned out, as Bea already knew, that "no real harm" is no different than harm.

Eli was married. Bea and Eli's wife, Marianne, were friendly when they stood next to each other at lawyerly cocktail parties. They discussed beaches and Cape Cod and rash guards. Eli went to get drinks and Marianne rested her hand on the arm of Monroe Nehemiah Clarke, a good man tending to his dying wife, and Bea did notice that she wanted to brush Marianne's hand away and then she turned her attention to Eli and the drinks.

Bea and Eli had been meeting at the Willowbrook Motel

for a few months. They lay back on the taupe chenille bed-spread, one evening after work, and they both sighed. Eli had given everything he had to give, in several positions, and they each drove home and Bea knew that she was just chasing pizza in a Chinese restaurant, asking for oranges in a hardware store (two different therapists, one for her marriage and one for this affair). Eli called before Bea could even take her coat off.

Marianne did not live through a long, awful illness. It was an aneurysm, and no one saw it coming. Eli, and everyone else, could not stop talking about how fit she was, about her half marathons, about her pescatarian diet and all the ways that she surely should have cheated death. Eli recited her last moments to everyone; her last moments as a woman on a bicycle had reported them to the paramedics, one of whom overshared with Eli before his senior, smarter partner told him to shut the fuck up. (Marianne fell to the ground, vomited, had a seizure, fell to the ground again, revived, and died.) After the funeral, at Eli's house, Bea is careful not to be too helpful, not to handle the china and the glasses like she knows her way around the kitchen, which she really does not.

Bea had a day of relief after Marianne died, with the affair having gone undiscovered (Bea called Gazala, who sighed and made it clear that she would have been happier if it had been Eli), and then she was ashamed of the whole thing. She stood in Eli's living room, admiring the pretty photo-on-canvas of Marianne in Hyannis, and silently apologized. With the absence of Marianne, it became clear, like

the white light of a winter morning, that Marianne had
never been the problem. Even Eli was not the problem.

Eli attends every possible workshop and program for
both grief and moving on, and it's easier, in the end, for him
to sell the house and move to Colorado, where his mother is,
than stay in the house with Marianne's many embroidered
pillows (first flowers, then abstracts, navy blue, light blue,
and white, Marianne's favorite palette) and her famously
white sofa, and wish that there was no Bea, that there were
no witnesses, except his grown son, who moves on so briskly
as to have disappeared around a corner, with a backpack,
never to return to Poughkeepsie.

It seems to Bea that she knows all of this, everything that
is to come, within twenty-four hours of Marianne's aneurysm, and by the time Bea is holding a palmier on a cocktail
napkin in Eli and Marianne's living room, on the first night
of shiva, she is ready to help Eli pack.

The only surprise comes in the last wave of women-
tidying-up Eli's living room and kitchen. Their dog, a corgi,
is at Eli's heels, and Eli is opening another bottle of wine.
Bea sees him kick the dog. Marianne loved that dog, the way
that dog people do and the way that people like Bea do not.
Bea sometimes saw dogs she thought were nice enough, or
handsome or even adorable (Anne's Norwich terriers, some
huskies and Bernedoodles), but a hobby that required her to
hold hot shit in a plastic-bag-covered hand and walk late at
night, in the foulest weather, was not for her. But Bea had
never kicked an animal in her life.

Eli, it turns out, has always hated Cookie. He says so. He

hated Cookie when Marianne brought her home from the
Norwich Terrier Rescue Society in Peekskill, and he never
stopped hating her. He told Bea this when they were at the
Hyatt in Poughkeepsie, while he was brushing his teeth. He
said that Cookie felt the same about him. She shat in Eli's
shoes. She peed on his side of the bed. She whined when he
and Marianne sat in front of the fire, on perfect winter evenings, with glasses of red wine and some snacks that Marianne had picked up as part of their endless, endlessly broken,
détente. Eli was not, as Bea knew, a bad man. Marianne had
not been a bad person, and Bea decided that she was also,
not bad.

"I'll take the dog," Bea said. Eli thought that this was a
sweet, pitiful effort to hold on to him, and Bea didn't argue,
but back in her own kitchen, with Cookie yearning for a
treat, paws up and head cocked, Bea knew that it was really
that her little house was empty and her heart emptier still
and that Cookie, with her foxy face and aristocratically de-
formed little legs, was just the ticket.

Even after all the Greats are gone, Lily's son, Harry,
grown and marvelous, internationally known and glamorous, sometimes wonders how, exactly, dear Bea (cousin?
aunt?) came to entwine her own white-bread life with mysterious, godlike Gazala and Samir, who seemed to have very
little need for the entwining that the other Greats did. His
own mother, cool and chill and also sometimes quite chilly
("Chilly Lily" is what Harry used to call her when talking to
his guide during his annual Vermont psilocybin session, and
the psilocybin seems to have helped him to stop calling her

that), has very little of the entwining inclination, but Bea
and his grandmothers, Honey and Anne, had made up for it
his whole life, bless them. Harry is very interested in how
people get where they want to be and who they want to be.

It was hard for Bea to watch Harry when he was little.
He was and remained one of her favorite people, and although no one, *no one*, knows this (but they do), she loves him
more than she loves anyone else. She used to think that
Harry was just a kindred spirit. (He was.) She thought, every
time she saw him, what a joy he is. He made her laugh, and
his tenderness and shamelessness delight her, then and now.
Also, at six, he read like a fiend, head down, feet up. Bea had
imagined herself being a good aunt to Harry, patient, fond,
and willing to retire when the time came, but when the time
came she knew much better.

When little Harry flung himself onto Bea, she draped
him round her neck like a stole and said, "Who wants this
old sack of potatoes?" Everyone at the table said: I'll take
some. When he raised his arms over his head, jazz hands
high, and said "I am magic!," Bea said: I'll give you magic,
and zerberted him on his tawny belly. Bea yearned for her
own Harry, and then stopped yearning, because she did love,
and was loved by, this Harry.

At those early dinners with the Greats, longing for more
love, Bea had sat with all her favorite people—not so much
the enviable and self-absorbed Lily (to put it more nicely, a
person entirely, apparently, complete by herself) but very
much Gazala and Samir, whom she'd chosen as her true
parents from the first day they'd met.

Later, and loved, Bea sees that she can be kinder to her late grandmother, who fed her and clothed her and paid for her braces, and to her long-dead parents, those reckless sweethearts, now that she's older than they were when they died. She still longs to see all three of them, to find some Cape Cod–adjacent Wakandan ancestral grove containing the kitchen of her childhood in her grandmother's house, with the shelf of curling cookbooks and the three cast-iron skillets and the big porcelain vase by the stove with whisks and wooden spoons in it, where we can have a decent cup of coffee and make sport of our neighbors (as her grandmother would have said), and her parents, still twenty-five and twenty-seven, would hold hands as the sun came down brilliantly through the kitchen window, clouds of pink and lavender, and she would fling her arms out to each of them, on top of the kitchen table, linking them.

And much later, when all the Greats are long gone and Harry is an international agent, representing actors and directors and chefs and soccer players, in his belted silk caftans and pink velvet suits and a mane of brown curls, Harry still visits his Aunt Bea, his A.B., whom he prefers slightly to his mother, which is more gratifying than either of them can say, and Bea and Harry drink apple cider old-fashioneds and play with Biscuit, who is the son of Brownie, who is the son of the Original Cookie.

Keeping On

Anne sits on a varnished oak bench thinking of all the benches she's sat on while waiting for judges and lawyers and clients. She runs her fingers over the wide whorled arm of the bench. This bench has probably been in the hallway since Anne was in law school, back when benches were massive, curvy slabs of wood made to be permanent and grand, decorating and serving fearsome, immutable justice.

She was not much impressed with the justice she'd seen for so many years, and she was not impressed by the current crop of benches on the second floor: green metal, designed to be uncomfortable, bolted to the floor as if anyone, homeless or otherwise, would carry one through the hall, past the guards, and down the marble stairs.

Retirement was easier than Anne had thought it would be. Possibly because (as Lily and Bea point out, often) she hasn't retired at all, she's just stopped working for the law firm that had finally put her name on the wall twenty years before. Anne loved the platonic ideal of law as much as any other child of immigrants would. She certainly didn't love lawyers as a breed, although she had really liked the two other old broads she palled around with (Yvonne Saperstein, also known as Big Tits, and Susie Sunshine, actually Sue-Ellen Munson, whose Southern accent came and went depending on the judge). And Anne had had real love for her mentor, Arthur Napoli, dead twenty years now, a soft-spoken, utterly mobbed-up old man who gave her a thousand cups of espresso and great advice on criminal cases and some clever ideas for civil ones. (He also told her that no law firm would make her a named partner until she was practically retired, and he wasn't wrong.) Now she calls Bea sometimes, and even better, Bea calls her.

But Anne did love justice, no matter how she got it, and she'd kept a .32 pistol in her house since 1974, just in case there was an opportunity to serve justice. When lockboxes became de rigueur, she got one and put it in her cedar closet, behind her big green parka. Two days a week now, Anne did her best to be the angel of justice, to be a Rolls-Royce of a lawyer for people who barely had bus fare and were coming to her through the Poughkeepsie Center for Women and Families.

Anne is waiting for Dorothea, who's never late. A little indecisive, a little slow to divorce, from Anne's point of view, but organized and smart and punctual. Dorothea is Surinamese by way of Amsterdam, married to an American she met if not in the red-light district then, as Anne understood it, very, very adjacent.

Anne bites her tongue while Dorothea debates about which door, with which tiger behind it, is better for her and her sons. Anne knows.

Dorothea, unnervingly tiny, not even five feet tall, with a stream of black hair, comes hurrying down the hall, her two American-size teenage sons right behind her. They love their mother. They slouch protectively, they move their baseball caps up and down their foreheads, scrolling through their phones, signaling indifference, manifesting love. Dorothea has a red bruise around her left eye, from her brow to the middle of her cheek. Anne opens the box of cookies she's brought from Gazala, the bakery (makes her smile, every time), and tells the boys to take the box, eat all the cookies, and leave Anne and their mother in peace for a few minutes. The boys take the box, mumbling their thanks, which seems to Anne, in this modern world, to be as good as doffing your hat in the old days. (Doffed? Is there a single person in the whole courthouse who even knows the word "doffed"?)

So, Anne says.

Dorothea puts her hand to the bruise and says: Let us proceed. She says that she has not made her way to Amsterdam and then to New York, has not serviced unappealing and unpleasant men, including her husband, so that she can wind up dead on her kitchen floor.

Agree, Anne says.

Also, Anne says, if you see that man's car in your driveway, or even across the street, or even on your block, you call 911. You tell them you have a protective order and you say

that he has threatened you and your minor children. You say
that you are not safe. You say that he may be armed.

Dorothea opens her mouth and closes it.

You lock every door, Anne says. You lock every window.

Dorothea nods. She calls the boys over, and, in the manner of boys, they hand the empty box back to their mother.
Anne gives Dorothea a side hug and nods at the boys, who
nod back.

See you in court as soon as we can, Anne says. Keep the
doors locked. No unregistered firearms in your house.

Tot ziens, Dorothea says. She stands on her toes and kisses
this fierce old lady on the cheek. The boys walk their mother
down the hall.

Anne calls Bea, before her next appointment. They talk
about Bea's cases.

Almost the Last Seder in Poughkeepsie

Poughkeepsie, New York
2014

April. Gazala and Samir love big spring. Unabashed. Sentimental and surprising, spring buries darkness and death in the green—not edited out, just resting. Not their time. The fat pointy rosebuds, not truly round, with their slightly darker ruffled edge making you forget the thorns, reddish and greenish, striking, not pretty. Little knives, glossy and effective. The house looks like it grew out of the ground. The moss around the bluestone, the tiny purple flowers edging the driveway and even inching into it, where they never weed. There is a faint green tinge to the white wood where the house joins the land, and that green tint has spread. Samir and Gazala stopped taking medications at a certain point, and they stopped power-washing the house around the same time. It is fine the way it is. It is, to them, as it should be. Everything coming together.

Anne and Alma were raised on Ashkenazic Seders. There'd been none at all for Honey, born United Church of

Canada and then Unitarian and now Jewish friendly and quietly witchy. Gazala and Samir knew about Seders only from the Cohens. Anne had brought a certain kind of Jewish American cuisine to Honey, and it was not, mostly, the good kind: matzoh balls from a mix, roast chicken (good one year, mummified another), egg matzoh from a box (Goodman's) or wheels of blistered matzoh from the Orthodox bakery in Brooklyn (Orthodox goniffs is what Alma said, and when Alma offers a criticism, no one argues the point). Before Richard's Alzheimer's got bad, Anne would ask Gazala if she could invite him, too, when he was between wives. Gazala always sighed and she always said yes, and she is glad now that she had said yes and she is a little sorry about the sighing. Richard was, really, a lesser version of Honey, and Honey is right here with her excellent posture, two seats down from Gazala, smiling warmly at Samir's explanations. A good addition to the family. Anne used to say of Richard that he was kind. Maybe. By Gazala's lights, Alma is the kind one. Alma is kind the way water is wet. It is her essence, but also, if the balm of her kindness is pointless, she knows how to turn another way and apply other pressure. Richard was smart. In the early years, he did tend to talk about Algeria, which pushed Samir into grim silence or, after a few brandies, to a certain kind of baiting. (Where did you read that? Long pause. Ah. By an Algerian writer? No? Long pause. Ah.) The times Richard did come, he would bring a spectacular red wine and a bowl of limp, gritty green beans, and Gazala cannot understand why this man, her late brother-in-law, as it was, whom she never liked much, who has been dead for some time, is absolutely haunting her Seder.

Gazala liked Harry since his birth. (Lily called Anne and said: I was going to take the chicken out of the oven but I can't because the baby's coming, and Honey and Anne arrived in minutes, more or less throwing Lily's husband out of the kitchen. Gazala and Alma got to the hospital by the time Harry was born. Richard came to the hospital that afternoon with balloons and the third wife.) Gazala likes most of Harry's friends. She also likes Lily's special friends—her throuple—Elizabeth and Shea, who are so American and non-Jewish and non-Algerian and non-French as to make Gazala's family look deeply cosmopolitan, and she does observe that every one of them, even Bea, who is averse to showing off, rises to the occasion, delivering airy bon mots and flinging up a hand, holding an imaginary cigarette.

Sometimes Anne brings lima beans as well. At one Seder, when Harry was very little, he'd looked at the lima beans and proceeded to throw handfuls of them to the ground. Lily gasped in shame, and Gazala looked at the floor for a minute. Then she said to Harry: Mon cher, go to the kitchen and get some paper towels, you can reach, and just scoop up those beans and toss them out. She made it sound like Harry was a born problem-solver, and Harry, who brooked very little authority in his young life, went, got, and scooped with great seriousness and then laid his head on Gazala's shoulder and she gave him a sip of champagne.

Lily liked to mix up the seating to suit herself, and once, a long time ago, she asked Alma to move a few seats away from

Izzy to make room for someone she, Lily, was dating. Izzy, shy and courteous, began to stand, as he would, and Alma put her hand on his shoulder. Anne watched her daughter across the table and laughed. Alma might be sorry after, she might make one of her gorgeous fruit pies to apologize for not moving, but as Alma said that night to adolescent Lily, when Lily was making her bring-down-the-patriarchy argument for Alma and Izzy to sit apart: We are one soul. Lily opened her mouth to argue, and Alma put up the flat of her hand. Sha.

Alma thinks of Izzy, of his kindness and his strength. Alma was a good person and she knew it, but Izzy had made her want to be better, to catch up to him, to shower him with thanks, and she does it still. She narrates events for him, even now. She remarks on what Lily is wearing and how tired Gazala looks. She tells no one, but she texts him, often, in the afterlife, and it is the thing that makes her appreciate cellphones. Izzy would smoke a cigar with Samir, the two of them quiet and content, and would bring his own perfect chopped liver and volunteer to carve anything that needed to be carved. (Anne said to him once: You are the Toscanini of carving. We should have a ham, even at Pesach, just for you. Izzy beamed. Compliments from his sister-in-law were not common.)

The haroset is a relief to everyone. Multiple versions flourish: There's haleg, from Iran, with date paste and walnuts and almonds mixed into a wet mass with cardamom and ginger and the usual cinnamon. Alma's charoset is traditional Polish haroset, with the sweet red wine that is disgusting in any other setting and the cinnamon and the honey, chopped chunky or as smooth as mortar. Bea, who cannot help herself, brings a Surinamese charoset for what will be Gazala's last Seder: It has cherry jam and coconut. Bea lays it on the table with a short speech about the Jodensavanne, the Jewish settlement in Suriname, whose inhabitants made their way hundreds of years ago under the Dutch, then the British, then the Dutch. People don't mind; they're curious about a dish that is not Middle Eastern and not European. Even Gazala takes a small spoonful and whispers to Bea: Parfait, chérie, and Bea does not care what anyone else thinks. She has brought a charoset that Gazala has deemed perfect and everyone else can just fuck right off.

Lily has brought fun Passover desserts: chocolate-covered matzoh, macaroons decorated with googly eyes and slivers of orange rind to make them look like roosters, candy for all the plagues: red Jolly Ranchers for the blood of the first-born, black licorice for blindness, Lindt eggs representing the cow-plague, about which there was a lot of discussion, as some people—Alma—feel that German candy still does not belong at a Passover table.

Bea did invite an old friend, who has had to cancel at the last minute, so Bea is on her own, within this family she's made her own, without herself having any Jewishness at all. (Bea used to contemplate converting, when she was younger, but she worried that Gazala might think converting was excessive and vulgar and that Lily, the Jewish Grace Kelly, might sneer. And then she didn't care.) Harry sits beside Bea, slipping her an Hermès scarf, a shockingly pretty, obviously expensive scarf of sunflowers. He has also, no fool, brought one, in a very different palette, for his mother. Gazala catches his eye and nods. Gazala gestures to Bea to come over, and Bea bends down so that Gazala can tie her scarf chicly and press her cheek against Bea's.

Seders have been at Gazala and Samir's big, beautiful, shambling house for years. As the kids said: Uncle Sammy and Aunt Gazala did not come to play, and they did not host in order to play second fiddle (as Samir put it, *the* second fiddle) to the Ashkenazi.

There are remarks in French and English (and side remarks in broken Arabic from Samir and further side remarks in Yiddish and Portuguese from Anne, who learns languages for pleasure).

They eat early, not at sundown, because Aunt Gazala hates to eat late. I'm not in Paris, she says, I can eat before nine.

Samir gives a short lecture, with each course, as if, despite all the years of these Seders, the guests would, with their stupid American minds, have forgotten all about the dates (*tamar*) and the way in which they represent a wish for peace. (You see: May it be Your will, God, that enmity will end. Bea, you see, ma chère, you see how *tamar*—the word for dates—resembles the word for ending: *yitamu*.) Bea nods happily, and when Samir indicates that it would be appropriate to bang the tabletop in agreement, Bea bangs the tabletop.

There are pomegranates, and it has been Lily's job, since she was six, to empty the halves of the pomegranates into a bowl of cold water and then, at the nearly last minute after Izzy's chopped liver has been put away and before the soup is served, to heap the seeds and the apple slices, sprinkled with lemon so they have no chance to brown, into small chipped porcelain bowls.

Samir instructs everyone: May we be as full of mitzvot as the pomegranate is full of seeds.

Before eating the apple slices: May it be Your will, God, to renew for us a good and sweet year.

Before eating the string beans (*rubia*) with slivered almonds and preserved lemon paste: May it be Your will, God, that our merits increase. (Samir: You see, dear Bea, dear girl, *rubia* resembles the word for increase: *yirbu*.)

Before eating the roasted pumpkin (*k'ra*): May it be Your will, God, to tear away all evil decrees against us, as our merits are proclaimed before You. (*K'ra* sounds like okra, but it has nothing to do with okra, and Samir points out that *k'ra* resembles the words for "tear" and "proclaimed.")

They make their way through beetroot (*selek*): May it be Your will, God, that all the enemies who might beat us will retreat, and we will beat a path to freedom. (And, here we go, *selek* resembles the word for retreat, *yistalku*).

None of these resemblances are obvious to anyone, but they know them by now and accept them, and also the odd similes and the Algerian and Yiddish mutterings, which go on and on. No one ever says to Samir: You are a French Algerian Jew, with no Jewish education at all, how do you even know Hebrew?, which is just as well because Samir learned everything he knows, and announces, from a Sephardic guide to Passover, published by a very, very small press in Schenectady, in 1959.

Before eating an absolutely perfect casserole of leeks (*karti*) that Gazala has put together while almost lying on top of the kitchen table, barely able to stand up from her back pain, which will turn out to be a tumor on her spine, and then will turn out to be benign but so tentacled and relentless that benign means nothing and Gazala will suffer through a dozen surgeries, dying with Alma by her side.

About the leeks: May it be Your will, God, that our enemies be cut off. (*Karti* resembles *yikartu,* the word for "cut off.") Samir says: Some Jews—Persians, I think—throw the scallions behind their backs and over their shoulders. And sometimes—and Samir shrugs approvingly—while they are tossing the leeks, the Persians recite the actual names of their enemies, of people they wish to *destroy*.

Bea gasps, as she does every time. Lily smiles. Harry claps. Oh *yes,* he says.

Samir says: Originally, we were supposed to use a fish's head or a sheep's head to symbolize our wish to be heads, not tails; leaders, not stragglers. Not goddamn sheep. (When Harry was little, was six, he laughed at the "goddamn" and, as was his lifelong habit, stood up on his chair, effortlessly, and cheered.) *Les moutons,* Samir says. The sheep's head reminds us of the ram that saved Isaac's life. He says: The Baghdadi Jews didn't use the fish head, just the sheep, because the word for fish in Hebrew, *dag,* sounds like the Hebrew word for worry, *d'agah.*

No one has ever heard Gazala criticize Samir, ever. No

one ever will. She does allow herself to smile and sigh during the Seder, shaking her head at all of this piety and Hebrew, neither of which interests her.

Samir looks at Gazala and shakes his head in a cloud of happiness, as if he'd lost track of the Seder. He lifts his wineglass to Gazala and then he says: Habibi, let's eat, and he winks at Bea, who melts, delighted even as a grown-up—as everyone is—when Samir takes notice.

Roses in October

Poughkeepsie, New York
2010

Bea has her own dear little house, her own garden, with
dahlias from Anne and hydrangeas from Samir, and sometimes she invites herself for a sleepover with Gazala and
Samir. A home visit, is how she thinks of it. With effort,
Gazala makes chicken with forty cloves of garlic, and Samir
and Bea make honey-glazed carrots and rice. No one has
dessert. After dinner, they each chew on a mango edible,
they listen to chaabi music, and Bea tucks them into their
beds. She washes the dishes and then puts herself to bed.

The moon is big and white, bright through the old curtains in Bea's little room. She hears gravel crunching. The
boxwood branches brush against the kitchen door. Bea's
door.

More footsteps on the gravel.

Bea puts on her shoes. She goes to the front hall closet.
She pushes aside Samir's three overcoats and Gazala's an-
tique Persian lamb jacket and her trench coat until she finds

Samir's cane. She puts on one of his overcoats and walks back to the kitchen. She unsheathes the cane and lays the sword on the table. Then she takes a hammer out of the utility closet and, armed, opens the kitchen door and steps outside onto the brick path. Her eyes adjust and she lifts the sword and the hammer.

She sees the back of a man, short and broad.

The man comes toward her, watch cap pulled down to his brow, fist upraised. His other hand reaches toward his pocket.

Bea turns sideways away from his fist and slashes him across the back of the hand and then across his cheek. The man yelps. *Bitch*. He glares and he weighs his chances and his potential reward and Bea swings her hammer and throws it at him. It hits his chest with a soft thud, and it's clear to both of them that she has not done any harm with the hammer. She slashes the air with the sword. The man looks at her one more time, shrugs, and lumbers off. Not worth it. He came for computers and jewelry in a house that seemed empty.

Bea goes back into the house, leaving her muddy shoes next to the kitchen door. She puts the hammer back into the utility closet, next to the jar of nails.

She puts the sword back into the cane and returns it and the overcoat to the front hall closet.

She boils water for tea. Her blood is singing.

The sun comes up and she sets the kitchen table for breakfast.

Not on my watch, you bastard.

After breakfast, Bea searches out Ruby Rose Harrison, psychic, recommended to Bea years ago. Ruby Rose Harrison is right there, on the internet, in Butternut, New York, where all the new hotels and cannabis farms are. Ruby Rose Harrison, as it turns out, had been an associate professor of anthropology, took psilocybin before it was all the rage, and left academia for a slightly derelict house on four beautiful acres in the Catskills. Bea kisses Gazala and Samir, and she gets into the car and drives to Butternut, New York.

Ruby Rose opens the door. She is serene and dark and also wearing scrubs, which Bea finds disturbing. Would there be blood? Exorcism? Why is it not possible for Ruby Rose to wear regular-person clothes?

Ruby Rose puts her hand out and Bea takes it and the handshake becomes Ruby Rose guiding Bea into an armchair across from hers, separated by a coffee table and a green shag rug. Ruby Rose's posture is perfect, like Grandma Isabel's.

Ruby Rose says, "You have roots but there have been disruptions. The trees are not flowering as you expected."

Bea starts to cry, much sooner than she expected. The roots must be her parents and her grandmother, and the damaged buds and branches must be her parents' bad driving and her grandmother's very old-fashioned parenting. The flowers must be that bad marriage, the stupidity with Eli, and the miscarriages that left her fragile and tough in odd places.

Ruby Rose looks remarkably uninterested in Bea's tears. She sits with her hands clasped and nods in the direction of the Kleenex box. "Would you like to do the cards?" she says.

Bea nods.

"Any particular deck?"

Bea feels like an idiot. She's a good researcher. She should have read up, but now she will choose some inappropriate or useless deck.

Ruby Rose doesn't smile, but her eyes soften. "There are a lot of decks," she says. "We can just use Rider-Waite. It's a classic."

"That sounds great. Who doesn't love a classic?"

Ruby Rose arches one thin eyebrow. There will be no banter here. She takes a deck of cards and passes it to Bea and asks for it back.

"Three questions," Ruby Rose says. "First question."

"My parents . . ."

"Which ones?" Ruby Rose says, laying down a cross of four cards. "Ah, ah, ah," she says. "The living or the dead?"

Bea looks at her.

Ruby Rose frowns as if Bea is the dumbest person she's ever read for. "Are you asking about your dead parents or your living ones?" she asks. "The white ones or the dark ones?"

"I don't know," Bea says. "My living parents?" she asks, but she knows who perfectly well and puts up her hand to stop Ruby Rose from ending the session in disgust. "Please," she says. "About my living parents. The dark ones."

Bea can see Gazala and Samir as clearly as if they are

sitting beside her. Gazala, unbreakable. Samir, unreadable, except for that faint bright thread of love that ties him to Gazala and connects him, loosely, probably, to Bea.

"Are they all right?" she says. "I mean, do they live a long time? I would like them to live a very long time."

Bea begins to cry, then wipes her face.

Ruby Rose smiles for the first time. "Well, you found them and they found you," she says. "Yes. They do not die young. Clearly." Ruby Rose gives a little snort, which is her laugh. "They are hundred-year-old rosebushes."

Bea says, "Maybe I'll be one too."

"Ah," Ruby Rose says, and she looks toward the Kleenex again. Then she picks up a card bright with a bird and stars and water. "Likely."

She picks up a few more cards, handling them like a magician, over and under her long fingers with dirt under the nails. She shakes her head. "I am sorry for the miscarriages. The last would have been a boy, you would have named him after your dead father. W?"

She touches two cards, side by side, upside-down. The Emperor and The Lovers.

"Ah, well. W—that's your father?—died terribly but he was not unhappy, and she, your mother, was very happy too that night. And before."

She gently picks up one of the upside-down cards. "They loved you."

Bea, like Samir, like Anne, has a good ear, and the longer Ruby Rose talks, the more Romanian she sounds.

"Are you Romanian?" Bea asks.

Ruby Rose puts the card down.

"I don't talk about me," she says, and Bea sees that there is a long whitish scar tracing Ruby Rose's hairline. "Next question?"

Bea asks if she will be happy. Happier than I am now, she says.

Ruby Rose picks up the cards and lays down three new ones. The one closest to Bea is a bunch of swords, jammed into a body on the ground, points first.

Ruby Rose says, "Let's see if there's something you can do to improve this current situation."

Bea starts to say, as has been her habit for years: No, it's okay, it's fine, and Ruby Rose looks like she wants to punch Bea in the face. Ruby Rose picks up the card with the swords and puts it down and picks it up again. She puts it down again and picks up a card with two sphinxes, riding forward, banner waving.

"Well, that's The Chariot. That's triumph."

Bea wonders what kind of triumph she can possibly have.

"You will triumph, you will move forward," Ruby Rose says. "It will take longer than you want." Her voice drops. "Longer than I would want for you, but it will come."

"Triumph?" Bea says.

"Love," says Ruby Rose, turning over a card with two lovers apart.

Ruby Rose cannot possibly be the name she was born with, Bea thinks.

"Rubin Rozeta," Ruby Rose says. "My birth name. Very similar, no?"

Bea nods, happy to be in the presence of the real thing. She looks at the Chariot card, a card, at least for her, of great and delayed and deep gratification. "How long do I have to wait?" Bea says.

Ruby Rose puts her dry hand, with knobby silver rings, tourmalines and agates, on every finger, atop Bea's hand. "I can't see," she says, "but when it comes, it is wonderful. It is everything you hoped for."

After the not good marriage and the stupid affair, after the night Bea attacked the man outside Gazala's house, after the afternoon with Ruby Rose, Bea steps into the next day as if the last twenty years have been a momentary lapse.

Bea decides to live for love, however long it lasts, and for children, whoever they belong to, and she never says a harsh word to or about Lily again. She embarks on what you could call a torrid affair with Monroe Nehemiah Clarke, her by-now-widowed colleague. Monroe made her laugh. She made him laugh. They worked well together. One day, after they'd mediated for two terrible, scheming parents and worked up a custody agreement that gave an unusual amount of child time to a kind and sensible aunt with money, they went out to an early dinner to celebrate. On their second martini, Bea put her chin on the back of her hand and flirted. Monroe opened his eyes, playfully (Oho, he said), finished his whiskey, and said: Let's take our time.

Envision a relationship between people, not young, feeling deep passion and attraction, in which intercourse is sometimes impossible, given some medical problems, and marrying does seem out of the question because Monroe has a son who worships his late mother and has a chilly contempt for all other women, including his own wife, and perhaps Gazala and Samir will not approve, and perhaps Bea will make a fool of herself, and she texts Harry, and then Lily, to tell them about Monroe. Gazala already knows. Gazala had met Monroe ten years ago, and she knew then but Bea didn't listen.

It will turn out that a happy life is not out of the question, and this love with Monroe frees Bea to be exactly who she was meant to be, sans rules, sans edicts, sans filter, and if it has made her a bit of a landmine on some occasions (not Gazala, perhaps, but not *not* Gazala), she is happy to be who she is. She is grateful. As she inches up on old age, she's glad that she had parents who loved her and a grandmother who did protect her from harm and she has had Gazala and Samir and Harry too.

Bea stands at her sink while Monroe, beside her, brushes his teeth and runs his hand over the back of his neck and that's all it takes. She tears up. He suggests that it would be better if she handled the clippers for him, and she takes them as if they were a diamond necklace. She dusts the little hairs off the back of his neck and rests her lips on his shoulder and Monroe closes his eyes in happiness.

Monroe Nehemiah Clarke lies next to Bea Frances Greene eating pear jelly beans. The man has a serious sweet tooth, and there is no dessert, in any form, from any country, he will not try at least once, chocolate over citrus, please, and no yogurt. He is all sweetness with Bea, almost always, and he wants sweetness from her. He has had problems and made problems and he has had peace lately, and what he wants in these last decades, what he hopes will be decades, is sweetness, is kindness, is pleasure. He calls her Sweetie. When they make love, he calls her Sweet Angel. Sweet. Angel. Two things Bea never knew herself to be. There is very little sharpness in him when he is with Bea. (She thinks there may have been quite a bit, in the past, with other people, but it has softened or it is resting now.) When he is annoyed with Bea, when she has brought up something he would prefer not to do or discuss, he begins, always, by saying, "Sweetheart," and his voice drops lower on the second syllable. She hears that tone and she doesn't mind. It is a little salt with the sweet. That's Monroe. Bea knows.

And while Bea rests her head on Monroe's thick shoulder, her hand on his bald head, his hand on her cheek, they tell each other stories of their childhood. Bea imitates her grandmother, in her finest moment, imitating Danny Kaye, stumbling faster and faster over *The pellet with the poison's in the vessel with the pestle, the chalice from the palace has the brew that is true* while tap-dancing with great seriousness. Monroe imitates his father's fierce spine and quiet power, telling his boys to stay out of fights—but if there must be a fight, come home. Whatever you have to do, come home. Monroe laughs until he tears up when he tells Bea how his mother would demand that his father beat the living daylights out of Monroe for some wrongdoing and how when his father, work-weary and disinclined, would eat his dinner and read his newspaper and finally, slowly, take Monroe into the living room and slowly unbuckle his belt, his mother would throw herself across the room, wailing like a Fury, and beg Monroe's father not to touch one hair on the blameless head of her beloved Monroe.

Beloved Monroe. Beloved Bea.

Monroe presses his face against Bea's, their noses touching, and she sees those banners snapping, she hears the horse galloping free of the chariot, and she sees little birds flying. She has it all.

Lying in bed with Monroe, rubbing his crisp gray chest hairs between her fingers, flicking his chubby earlobes while he reads the news on his phone, Bea laughs out loud, remembering her unfortunate marriage and the embarrassing affair, and now she thinks: Thank you, guys, I couldn't have done it without you. She thinks of Gazala and hopes very hard that she died happy. Not just glamorous and unexpectedly tender and fucking spectacular, but as happy as Bea is now.

I miss her already, Bea says.

Monroe lifts his reading glasses toward the ceiling, a salute. Of course. Her memory will be a blessing.

All of their memories, Bea says. I think the Greats are going to fall like dominoes.

PART THREE

Always

The Family

The Light

The green and yellow light comes through the leaves of the big linden tree in the middle of the front lawn. She has seen this tree from her bedroom window, from the patio, from the living room, every day, every year. She sees it now, huge and flaming gold.

Her father sits under it, reading the paper, sipping his tea, and she sits beside him on the grass. Her mother walks past, holding hands with another woman. It must be Samir's mother, who died just after bringing her baby into this world. He smokes. He puts his hand on her cheek and she feels the heat of it. She smells his cigarette—The Balkan Sobranie Cigarettes, Made from the Finest Yenidje Tobacco, in the white tin.

Madame pours mint tea into the red glasses.

Samir offers a Sobranie to Mr. Cohen, and the men sit on the fire escape of the Cohens' apartment talking and smoking. Alma has just met Izzy Taubman and she is, sud-

denly, beautiful. Si belle. Alma tells them that Izzy has proposed, and she and Anne kiss Alma, big red kisses right on
her cheek and forehead. The men come back in through the
window. Mr. Cohen opens the schnapps he keeps under the
sink. Everyone toasts everyone around the kitchen table.

Anne and Honey sit on the couch, Anne's sturdy, dim-
pled hand in Honey's long, elegant one, and they hold each
other's hands so tight that their knuckles whiten, and they
tell everyone what everyone already knows and she is glad
for them and, only for a breath, sorry not to have had that
moment.

They are in bed in Oaxaca. The curtains move a little.
There is enough breeze so that they do not suffer, not so
much that the little pool of sweat on his chest evaporates,
not so much that she needs to pull up the cotton blanket.
They share a cigarette, which they never do. They whisper,
in French, so that no one will hear them.

Levons Nos Verres

Poughkeepsie, New York
2015

It's too much.

These two middle-aged women, Bea and Lily (still girls to the remaining Greats, and they get to be girls until there are no beautiful, failing old ladies to call them girls), sit in Gazala and Samir's house, in the long living room with all the windows, all ten now spotty and streaked with winter. Samir cannot find the name of the window cleaners, and Gazala was not available.

Bea and Lily look out the cleanest window and see Honey, Anne, and Alma on the patio, dragging the wicker furniture onto the lawn with difficulty. Laughing. All three of them have tossed their sweaters and fleece vests onto the ground. They are drinking shandies and popping pretzel sticks. It is the first warm day. Samir has probably gone up for a nap. He rests now, all the time, in Gazala's bed. Bea brought him some Brazilian lemonade, and Samir said it was the best thing he ever drank. Bea is now in charge of

Brazilian lemonade. Lily was in charge, Lily felt, of bringing all of Gazala's jewelry, all three wooden boxes and even the big necklaces on the maple jewelry stand (It holds the junky pieces, Gazala had said; you don't put anything of value on it), down to the dining room table. They put down the embroidered Mexican tablecloth so they can make piles and not scratch the table. Everything Gazala had went to Samir, as they had discussed, although he always expected that he would go first.

The night after Gazala's death, Samir sits with the other Greats and muses: I can die now. I do not need to live. I do not care to live. The women say nothing. If there had been a young person, a person under seventy, in the room, that person might have piped up that Samir was loved, that they all need him and would miss him terribly, that they all want him to stay.

No one says that.

Samir tells Lily and Bea that all the pottery and jewelry is theirs to keep: to share or to sell. He gestures to the dining room table where they'll divvy things up and goes back to his nap in Gazala's recliner.

The remaining Greats have already declared themselves. None of them want anything.

It's all for you girls, Anne says.

Alma smiles and nods. I mean, where are we going? Us old ladies? To the opera?

Honey says: We could, we should go to the opera before we cork off. But we don't need to be all dolled up.

Bea thanks them.

Bea makes two shandies, and they toast Gazala after the Greats have gone to bed.

Levons nos verres, Lily says.

Bea raises her glass.

Also, Bea says, to us.

Lily raises her glass again. Damn right.

Gazala's funeral is not like Honey's Dead People's Party. Honey has felt fine since then (mostly), and she makes it all the way through Gazala's funeral, more or less.

They all make it through. Although not for much longer.

Everyone is a worn-out, wet-faced, but unmistakable version of themselves in the lovely, long living room. Thirty rented white chairs crowd behind the three teal velvet armchairs. Samir is silent and shattered, carrying the bits of himself around in a black suit, with scuffed black shoes, drooping black socks, his faded black shirt with a wide black tie from the eighties. Gazala wasn't there in the morning to say, *Non, non, non, et absolument jamais.* The other women pat him, dust him, bring him tea he doesn't drink and food he doesn't eat. The children of Gazala's favorite hairdresser and the nearest neighbors and Samir's favorite floor manager come. Lily's people, Elizabeth and Shea, come as guests and also as caterers. None of these people (the young people, as the old people will call them forever) have ever seen Samir as anything except implacably distant with moments of charm and they all keep their distance. At one point, Samir lifts a hand to pat Bea as she goes past. She's fussing over the best seating for the oldest people. (The Greats are by no means the oldest people here today.) Bea holds on to Samir's hand and presses it to her chest, eyes streaming. She stops walking and stands there until Samir lets go. Monroe goes around her and seats two old men who look like they may not get even as far as the white chairs.

Anne and Alma sit on either side of Samir, in piles of dark gray topped with patterned silk scarves, and Honey sits behind him, in a black jacket, black trousers, and burgundy cowboy boots. Her big hands rest on his shoulders for the entire service. Anne can barely sit up, she is so tired, and Honey pats Anne from time to time. Alma, as is her habit, silently tells Izzy everything. (Oh, see that, that's the dentist. *The* dentist. He's still handsome, you can't argue, but it was not a good idea. We can say that.) None of them wanted to speak, so the rabbi, or rabbi-like person, brought in by Bea just yesterday, does the heavy lifting for the family, for all of them, with some general but accurate remarks and some cantorial singing that pleases everyone with its oddness and ululating. Harry has come, dressed somewhere between the youngish Oscar Wilde and Sam Smith. He's with his new partner, Ty, equally handsome and dressed in a spectacularly somber and beautifully cut suit, a thousand shades of black with black John Lobb oxfords. They both wear eyeliner (A mistake, Harry says later, having to wipe his eyes all day), and they both hug and hold Harry's aunts, and even his mother, Lily, as if they are the most precious people on earth. As they are.

The little service is at the house, and bouquets are put in

the kitchen until Lily pulls herself together to arrange them. Without discussion, Bea and Lily throw the mums, carnations, and wilting roses into the trash, as Gazala would have instructed. The memorial service is in French, English, and Tuareg, the only thing Samir insisted on. He didn't care who spoke, what music was played, what plates were used, or if there was wine or just coffee and tea. He refused to discuss things.

With families, everyone is a time traveler. If anyone in the room knew you before you were exactly who you are right now, they still see you as you were, and as you are. You are your own double, or even triple, your toddler self flinging the mashed potatoes, your teenage self refusing to eat the potatoes (or dairy or beef or foods not native to the area), and you may even catch glimpses of yourself ten years ago, that night you were angry with your spouse, skipped dinner, and finished the evening with a nightcap and some flirtatious second cousins.

Honey will get to see everyone, here and gone, on this chilly April day. Passover would be very soon, what the girls would have called early, which Honey now knows means before Easter, whenever Easter comes. It is not yet the fat, green, grabby heart of spring, that time of year that Gazala and Samir were mad for, him in the garden, her in the house putting pots of hyacinths on every sill. The little creek behind the barn is just rising to the grasses, and some children should be splashing in it, muddy and delighted. The scholar tree near the patio unfurls its leaves, green on top and bluish underneath. The two stands of birches are recovering from winter, all white and gray, with yellow-green slips at the ends of the thin branches. In the fall, Honey will sprinkle some of Samir's ashes, as he asked, at the base of the birches, after the rest of the ashes are divided into urns for Bea, for Lily, for Alma and Anne. In the winter, Honey will give an urn of Anne's ashes to Alma and another one to Lily. The following summer, Lily and Shea will toss Alma's ashes around the Lakewood chicken coop, among the Rhode Island Reds and the Light Brahmas. Honey will keep Anne's ashes in a ceramic box in her bedroom and sprinkle a handful among the red dahlias in the summer.

Gazala is gone, but Honey sees her in every room. (*Many great dears are taken away, What will become of you and me . . .*) She sees Gazala right now, the first time they met, looking at Honey from behind her sunglasses, lounging in the big wicker chair still on the patio, splintering even then. Honey approved of the fact that Samir threw nothing out. Use it up, wear it out, make do or do without, her father always said. Anne and Alma were a big, sisterly pair and Gazala and Samir were another big pair, wired together, of course, and Honey and Samir were an odd, persistent, unseen little pair. When they were both in the pantry, or in the hall, they always smiled broadly at each other or saluted, like long-lost friends happily surprised. If Honey had married a man, she would have wanted a man like Samir: silent, competent, capable of great charm and a little menace, a titanium rod underneath the puttering and the old clothes. Samir could not ever even imagine another woman, but in another world, in an imaginary Algeria, with France and Gazala vanished dreams, he feels he could have lived with Honey, two quiet horticulturalists. (He has three of her lilac prints, framed, on his wall, next to his postcard of Kherrata.) They would live together on a vineyard outside Oran and she would be an easy companion to him and an affront to his Algerian neighbors, in her pale blondness, and this would amuse them both.

Ah, the ladyfriend, Gazala had said when Anne first brought Honey over. She took an impossibly long drag on her cigarette and smiled up at the sky. One slim trousered leg over the arm of the chair. She put her martini glass down on the bluestone. She patted the frayed cushion on the loveseat near her.

I am afraid I know nothing of the Midwest, Gazala said. She waved her hand toward the green lawn, making a point.

Anne walked over to Gazala and looked down at her.

I love her, Anne said.

Gazala sighed. Of course. Forgive me. She took off her sunglasses. She said to Honey: You make my sister happy and I love you already.

That seemed unlikely to Honey but she would not argue with Gazala. She argued lightly with Samir, for more than sixty years, because they understood each other so well.

Honey pictures Anne, that first time, that first day, that day when Richard was away and light streamed across their bodies and her hands shook and the two of them astonished themselves from Lily's bedtime (Anne, sitting with Lily for

forty-five minutes, reading *The Poky Little Puppy* until Honey
thought she would weep) until little Lily called out in her
sleep at three A.M. (And Honey still remembers jumping out
of the bed—Stop, drop, and roll—dressing on the floor and
running on tiptoe down the hall to the guest room and thinking: Is this what it will be? This?)

And here is nineteen-year-old Lily, lying on the bed, face
buried in a big pillow, weeping hard that she failed her aikido test in France, and even though everybody there was
pretty well-behaved and the doshu was strict, they were all
laughing at her. In French. Don't tell my mom, do not, Lily
said, and Honey said: All right, for now.

Bea sits near Elizabeth and Shea, Lily's people. They are
the new green shoots in this old log, and they have brought
their little boy, Ryan, who is just becoming a person. Ryan
sits in Bea's lap while flirting with Lily (it occurs to Bea and
Lily that this is not a bad system they've developed over the
years) and sucking on his own hand. Ryan cannot stop staring at Harry, and Harry notices Ryan too. Harry will be
more Mick Jagger than Puck, weathering like a man on a
yacht, a wiry and fit old man in ways that require yoga, car-
dio, and vegetables. And Harry has all the moves and always
will, and he has Ty, and they have just begun to talk, dream-
ingly, about whether there might be a little Harry or Ty (or
Ryan) in their future. And Harry drums his fingers on the
table, watching Ryan (chubby and laughing, with the map of
Ireland on his face) intently, and Bea sees wonderful little
Harry, as he once was, standing on that table and singing
"Proud Mary." And Bea bounces Ryan.

Harry says: After dinner, a dance party (Harry impersonating Tina Turner, who taught Mick Jagger everything), and Ryan says, Yeah yeah.

The memorial's not until tomorrow.

"I don't think she'd have liked the food we have," Lily says.

Bea runs her fingers over a string of turquoise beads.

"These are your color, for your eyes," Bea says. "Your brioche is amazing. Elizabeth and Shea are very nice."

Lily smiles and plays with a wide jade bangle, the stone so closely wrapped in gold wire that it's barely visible.

"I really like Monroe," Lily says. "Anyway, people don't come for the food."

Bea laughs and then Lily laughs.

"Well, Jews," Lily says.

They look up at the long shelves of the matte black pottery.

"That's a lot," Bea says. "She loved it."

Lily said, "You know who'd like it, I think?"

Harry, Bea says.

He loves a collection, Lily says.

They smile about Harry.

How 'bout this, Bea says. We each take one, because I think we'll be sorry if we don't, and we give the rest to Harry, we can tell him tomorrow, and he can open a gallery, or fill up a place in the Catskills, or whatever amazingness he wants.

Agree, Lily says. I'll take a lantern.

Me too, Bea says.

We can leave the rest up on those shelves, I think, for now.

Agree, Bea says, and she starts to get up.

Come on, Lily says, let's just finish.

Bea opens the top drawer of the biggest jewelry box. She takes out a small gold badge, an insignia, the map of France with the Cross of Lorraine on it.

"It's the symbol for the Free French."

Oh, Lily says. It seems to her now that she could have passed her aikido tests in some dojo in Manhattan and done molly on weekends and it's Bea whom they should have sent to France, to explore and become.

In a drawer by itself is a brooch, a fat pale-blue-almost-lilac flower carved from something heavy, smooth and opaque, resting on a scrap of black velvet. They don't know what it is. (Chalcedony with a cabochon sapphire, five spikes of four diamonds each, and gray gold. Suzanne Belperron made two, one for the Duchess of Windsor. Here is the other.)

I don't know what to do with that, Bea says.

(A few years later, Bea will wear the pin, for luck, on her best black suit for the New York Supreme Court, and a very chic woman will stop Bea in the courthouse hall and say: Oh my God, Belperron.)

Me neither, Lily says. Let's just start with the stuff where we at least know what the hell it is.

They sip another round of shandies and get down to it, until it's so dark in the house that they turn on the lights, and they eat snacks, wipe their hands, and sort every ring, bracelet, and necklace. The other Greats have gone to bed, Harry and Ty have rented an Airbnb that had promising photos, just a mile away, and the grown children of the remaining friends have also driven home, their elderly mothers in the backseats, quiet except to thank their children for the driving.

Honey makes her way upstairs to Samir's bed and thinks of herself as not so much alive, these days, as not yet dead. It's fine. She does, sometimes, wonder how many more Seders, how many more roast chickens, how many more evenings ahead without her people, but there is still the bond with Lily, of course, and with Harry and now Ty, who looks forbidding but is the most crème brûlée of all of them, glittery crust above, sweet vanilla custard beneath. And Ty has brought a woman with him, whose name Honey missed and whose connection she has not grasped. (It is Ty's recently widowed sister, about whom everyone knows only what Harry has shared: No kids. Husband died climbing a mountain. Self-absorbed. Don't get too attached.) Honey sees Lily carrying the platter of roast chicken and smashed potatoes at the last Seder that Gazala and Samir had—and she sees Izzy Taubman, God bless him, standing up for his big moment, carving the enormous chicken, and Alma glowing with pride as everyone then says: Oh, Izzy, you know how to carve, you really do. And right behind Izzy, Honey sees Lily making peace with Bea, laying her hand softly on Bea's shoulder, everyone flirting with that redheaded baby with the Irish name. She thinks of Samir, down the hall, and wonders, without worry, if he will die while they are all in the house or if he will wait until they have left the house empty, which she knows he hopes they will do, and soon.

After the memorial, in the late afternoon, Harry pops up and raises his glass. To my people, Harry says. Wherever I go, I know that I have a home, and my home is with all of you. Gazala and Samir: *Adieu, mes chéris, mes lumières* (and no one says: Samir is not yet dead), you remain my standard of elegance and tenacity. And to the fabulous Cohen girls, the biggest hearts, the strongest souls, we can hardly bear to be without you all. To Honey, please, God, long may she wave over us (he raises his glass to the ceiling), and to all of us, still here, and thank you, thank you, to Lily and Bea, who will steer the ship so beautifully.

And Lily and Bea dab their eyes.

Lily lifts her glass of club soda to Harry. Bea passes Ryan back to his father and takes Monroe's hand. She is lit up with him, with holding his hand in front of her family and right in front of people she doesn't know very well (a few other surviving shopkeepers of Poughkeepsie, still mobile; the home healthcare aide; Gazala's dentist, still handsome at eighty-five).

Monroe, Bea says, glowing, would you like a glass of wine?

Monroe's dimple deepens and he says that he would, and he says: Let's go get a few more bottles. Let's go to the pantry.

In the pantry, with the stacked tins of smoked mussels

and smoked clams and white anchovies, a two-pound sack of dried apricots, six bags each of Soldanza Bananitos and Maduritos, there is a case of white and a case of red and one large framed photograph on the wall, the same one Bea has in her office and Lily has in the bakery. Anne is on one side, Alma on the other, Gazala in the middle, all three in white blouses and black pleated skirts and ballet flats.

Monroe kisses Bea, and Bea cannot let him go. She takes his hand, to bring him to Samir, who will shake Monroe's hand and hold Bea in his arms for a long time.

Beatrice, he will say. Yes.

Samir makes his way upstairs and lies down in Gazala's bed, wrapping her heavy red rebozo around him.

You are my life, he says to her.

Oh, I know, she says. You are mine.

Acknowledgments

Many thanks, and even more, to my editor, Kate Medina, tireless captain, the most appreciative and astute of readers.

My agent, Claudia Ballard, is wise, kind, and fierce, very good all around and great in tight spots.

All my love to my early readers and dear friends who put up with and improve my pages and my life: Bob Bledsoe, Tayari Jones, Valerie Martin, Julia Reidhead, and Kate Walbert. And, most especially for this book, my daughter Sarah Moon, a true friend and a (very) good writer.

For their support, wit, and depth of insight in all things, I thank my son, Alexander Moon, and my daughter Caitlin Moon Sorenson.

I want to thank and praise my Greats: Raisele and Davide Pajus, Frieda and Isadore Rosen, and Malcolm Keith.

Judith Thurman's *Secrets of the Flesh: A Life of Colette* was a constant companion, as were Alan Riding's *And the Show Went On: Cultural Life in Nazi-Occupied Paris,* Maurice Goudeket's *Close to Colette: An Intimate Portrait of a Woman of Genius,* Mouloud Feraoun and James D. Le Sueur's *Journal, 1955-1962:*

Reflections on the French-Algerian War, and Umm Maryam's *A Kitchen in Algeria.*

For much of the research required, I thank the incomparable Sterling Memorial Library of Yale University and the incomparable research skills of Jon Logan-Rung.

I appreciate, as always, over the decades, the thoughtfulness, determination, and astonishing range of talents of my assistant, Jennifer Ferri.

About the Author

AMY BLOOM is the author of four previous novels: *White Houses, Lucky Us, Away,* and *Love Invents Us;* and three collections of short stories: *Where the God of Love Hangs Out, Come to Me* (finalist for the National Book Award), and *A Blind Man Can See How Much I Love You* (finalist for the National Book Critics Circle Award). Her first book of nonfiction, *Normal: Transsexual CEOs, Crossdressing Cops, and Hermaphrodites with Attitude,* is a staple of university sociology and biology courses. Her most recent book is the widely acclaimed *New York Times* bestselling memoir *In Love.* She has written for magazines such as *The New Yorker, The New York Times Magazine, Vogue, Elle, The Atlantic, Slate,* and *Salon,* and her work has been translated into seventeen languages.

amybloom.com
Facebook.com/AmyBloomBooks
Instagram: @AmyBethBloom

About the Type

This book was set in Baskerville, a typeface designed by John Baskerville (1706–75), an amateur printer and typefounder, and cut for him by John Handy in 1750. The type became popular again when the Lanston Monotype Corporation of London revived the classic roman face in 1923. The Mergenthaler Linotype Company in England and the United States cut a version of Baskerville in 1931, making it one of the most widely used typefaces today.